# MANDVI

The interwoven stories of five women.
A complete saga of life, loss and love.

*Nilu A*

INDIA • SINGAPORE • MALAYSIA

# Notion Press

No.8, 3rd Cross Street
CIT Colony, Mylapore
Chennai, Tamil Nadu – 600004

First Published by Notion Press 2020
Copyright © Nilu A 2020
All Rights Reserved.

ISBN  978-1-64983-889-6

# CONTENTS

Contents

Dedicated to my beloved mother

SALMA OSMAN ABOOSALLY

# Acknowledgement

To my dear husband Zarkir, who after learning of my facination with a mystical place called Mandvi, took me there to visit in 2017.

To my beloved children, who have always encouraged and supported me in every endeavour.

# PART ONE

# MANDVI

Mandvi is a coastline town in Kutch district in the Indian state of Gujarat.

It was once a major port in the region and served as the summer resort for the rajas of Kutch.

The old city was enclosed within the fort wall, the remains of which can still be seen today.

The town has a four-hundred-year-old shipbuilding industry and still builds small wooden ships.

It is famous for its beaches, the Vijay Vilas Palace, Rukmavati bridge, Mazar-e-Nooruddin, the tomb of Syedna Noor Muhammed Nooruddin, 72 Jinalay Jain Temple, and Shyamji Krishna Varma Smarak monument.

# CHAPTER 1

# SURYA CHANDNI TAARE / 2017
# "A STAR IS BORN."

It was down to the five finalists and the final question from the judges.

"If you were crowned the winner today, where in this world would you choose to go, and why?"

"Mandvi, India," she replied.

"Since you are the only contestant to choose a specific place, in your own country, I would very much like to know the reason," asked the judge who had posed the question.

"It is a place where my beloved late grandmother grew up and spoke so fondly of, I have a longing to trace my roots," she answered.

Eventually, the drumbeat rolled, trumpets were sounded, and the winner was announced.

The New Miss World 2017 was "Miss India, Surya Chandni Taare MacLachlan."

## MANDVI, INDIA

Mehul Jadeja was not particularly feeble, although quite elderly now, but he moved slowly using a walker after the stroke he had. He lived by himself in his old ancestral home, looked after by a few loyal domestic helpers. He spent his days sticking to a rigid routine which included time for reading, meditating, yoga, and, as was his habit, watching the national news programme at seven every evening.

It came on as the headline that evening. The new "Miss World, Miss India." This would not have been of much interest to him under normal circumstances, but she drew his immediate attention. There was something so familiar about her that it intrigued him. He had only known one other who had possessed those strangely shaped eyes. He listened to her interview and heard her mention Mandvi, and when she put her hands together in the traditional Indian gesture, he saw an unusual but distinctive bracelet adorning her slender wrist.

He moved slowly to an old desk and pulled out an album. There, in it, were some photographs he had taken many years ago. Although in black and white, the prints were still clear and the resemblance quite startling. Looking like a startled doe, her strangely shaped eyes wide-open, dressed in wedding finery was his sister and, on her wrist, the very same unusual but distinctive bracelet.

Long lost memories flooded back. He needed to have answers. He picked up the phone to call his son in Ahmedabad, but changed his mind and dialled his grandson instead.

## KARACHI, PAKISTAN

Sheikh Zaaheb sat in his wheelchair amidst a circle of associates in deep conversation. Although injured and immobile now, as the former head of this organization his words still carried weight. He cut a magnificent figure. A large man in his signature pure white cotton kurta, a hand-woven woollen shawl draped over his broad shoulders, with his once-famous red-gold mane now turned white-gold with age. The only adornment he ever wore was a locket on a thick chain around his neck. The locket was almost as much of a legend as he was. Some said it contained a poisoned needle, others said a cyanide capsule, but many believed that he wore it as a good luck charm or a reminder since it had stopped an assassin's bullet.

Today, his words were often drowned out by the loud raucous comments arising from the adjoining room, where his young and boisterous grandson was watching the pageant on television with a group of his friends. The old man smiled indulgently, he understood. After all, every hot-blooded young man loved looking at beautiful young women.

Suddenly, the whistles and cheering turned to angry loud tones. He heard the words "India, Muslim, haram" coming from the next room. He wheeled himself there to see what was causing the commotion and then, he saw her. The Miss World 2017.

A blast from the past. She floated gracefully down the ramp for the victory parade. A vision in a long flowing gown. Her hair swept up. Her strangely shaped eyes seemed to look straight at him. She raised one arm to hold up her crown, and then he saw it, that beautifully hand-crafted, distinctive bracelet adorning her delicate wrist.

## SCOTLAND

Rowan Andrew MacLachlan was seated at the head of the vast oak dining table, a full breakfast laid out before him. He sipped his morning tea thinking how it was that the tea was never as good as he remembered it to be.

The old stone castle was lively this weekend. His fifteen-year-old daughter had invited a few of her friends over to stay. They were, as usual, watching television in the living room and, at first, her loud shrieks of "no way, no way" did not disturb him. Suddenly, she came tearing into the room followed by her friends, saying "Pa, do any other MacLachlans exist outside of Scotland?"

He was amused and curious. MacLachlan was an unusual Scottish name and he personally did not know many who still carried that name.

"Come Pa, you have got to see this MacLachlan," she said, dragging him by his hand into the next room. He saw this beautiful girl being interviewed on the television. "See Pa, the new Miss World, Miss India, Surya MacLachlan."

It could not be, it is not possible, he thought as he turned abruptly and hurried up to his office. There, in his safe, hidden at the back, he pulled out an old letter. A letter he had thought to be emotional blackmail, a letter he had not believed and had not acknowledged.

He was from an old, titled wealthy family. He knew the press; he feared the repercussions. He had to know, he had to make sure, he had to go back.

## COLOMBO, SRI LANKA

A wealthy matriarch now, Jameela had been blessed in life. A happy childhood, a kind and loving husband, wealth, health, and a happy family. The family had gathered together on her invitation this evening, her three children with their brood of offspring. It was, as usual, a loud and happy lot.

The large colonial bungalow was surrounded by well-tended gardens and manicured lawns. It was not unusual for the family to gather together, as it happened every few weeks upon someone's birthday, but today was not one of those celebrations.

She sat in her favourite chair in the opulent living room, a large flat-screen television broadcasting the Miss World contest. For once, the entire family sat around with interest. There was cheerful banter and some groans as the finalists were announced, the usual wagering which was a common practice in the family having taken place.

Jameela had been hoping for the girl's success but not really expecting her to win and she could not contain her excitement when the winner was finally announced. "I know her," she said, "I met her in Mumbai, on my last visit there."

It had been five years ago when she had received the letter from her childhood friend and flown to Mumbai to visit. The girl had just turned fifteen then. She remembered the tall, gawky young thing with the promise of budding beauty. She remembered the girl listening avidly to their reminisces on their childhood in Mandvi. After the demise of her friend, she had inquired after the girl and had been informed that she was living abroad. It was only when she won the title of Miss India that Jameela was made aware of her existence again.

As she had expected, she was now the centre of attraction, particularly among her young grandsons. She enjoyed the attention and promised that she would invite the girl over for a visit sometime in the future.

## NEW DELHI, INDIA

The party was in full swing; music blaring, champagne flowing. It was a celebration of her victory. There were a lot of loud jubilations and congratulatory back-slapping among his peers and employees. Although he was the host, Mr Lohan Mehta slipped away to his office on the top floor of the building and re-ran the recording for the fourth time that night.

He paced back and forth, watching her float down the stage, wearing the sash and the crown. Stunning, ethereal, she owed him everything. The stylists, the designers, and the trainers had all been hand-picked by him. He brooded over her post-victory interview. She had graciously thanked every one of them, the agency specifically, his mother particularly, but there had been no mention of him.

He had known from the moment his mother had introduced her to him that she was exactly what he had been seeking. Her unspoilt innocence was what he wished to mould into his ideal dream girl, the blank canvas on which he could create what he considered the picture-perfect partner for him.

He seethed with resentment. He had made her. She belonged to him. He realized that it was time to take matters into his hand, it was time to curb that independence, it was time to bring her to heel. As soon as she set foot back in India, it was time for 'a proposal.'

# CHAPTER 2

# BHOOMI / 1950 - 1970
# "SALT OF THE EARTH."

I was no beauty; 'pleasant,' 'a comfort to her mother,' were the kindest words I remember. I was born three years into my motherlands' newfound independence, in the small coastal town of Mandvi, India. A daughter, and an only child, I was a rarity in those times. Mandvi was a town that grew by a river bordering the sea. I lived near an old lighthouse in a small ramshackle house, four crumbling walls holding up a leaky thatched roof. My mother was my rock, my world. She was an enterprising woman who had used every opportunity she got to lift herself out of her hard life. She was born into a poor Muslim family, one of nine siblings who lived in a village on the outskirts of the town. The only reason, I felt, she had married my weak father was that he had inherited this small piece of land with the old shack. A place that gave her a way out, with a roof over her head.

My father was a thin, scrawny man with a wheezy cough, always moaning about "his lot in life." He spent his days lying on an old camp-cot, smoking rolled up beedis and complaining of his many imaginary ailments. Ailments which he used to excuse himself from any physical work. My mother had taught herself to sew and was a seamstress. A stout, strong woman, she used the only skill she possessed to fend for herself instead of depending on a whining husband. I took after my mother, both in appearance and nature, but by some quirk of fate, the only feature that I had inherited from my father, my long spindly fingers, held me in good stead in the years ahead.

As a child, for as long ago as I could recall, I accompanied my mother everywhere. It was many years later, on a rare visit to her village, that I heard from one of my aunts that this had not always been the case. As a baby, she used to leave me in the care of my father. Once, when I was a toddler of around three years of age, she had returned to find me naked, lying unconscious on the ground, bleeding, with a large swelling on my head. I was told that she had scooped me up in her arms and run many miles to the only medical practitioner she knew of and had ever been to in her life.

This kind man who practised native medicine had, with many a strange concoction and personal attention saved my life. He and his good wife had kept me in their own home for many days and kept me from death's door.

I cannot remember the incident and I never learnt how I suffered the injury, but as far as I can recall, I accompanied my mother everywhere. My earliest childhood memories are of my mother pedalling on old sewing machines, in pokey little rooms or narrow verandas, while I played quietly by myself at her feet.

Three families in Mandvi played pivotal roles in my life.

In my early years, my mother, ever grateful to the doctor who had saved my life, visited his home to sew for his wife. The doctor lived in a modest house close to a famous Bohri shrine in the town. Both Dr Amir and his dear wife took a personal interest in my health, diet, and well-being. They had two sons, Ahamed and Saif, aged around twelve and nine at the time. They were boisterous and rough but they were the closest I had ever been to having siblings. These visits were the only times from my childhood that I remember fondly. I remember running around, playing games, and shrieking with laughter. They were good people, kind and caring. This was the only house where I did not have to sit quietly entertaining myself while my mother was busy sewing.

By the time I was in my teenage years, I had acquired my mother's ability of cutting out and stitching garments, but in one skill I surpassed her. My thin spindly fingers helped; I excelled; I could embroider exquisitely. It was this talent that brought me to the attention of the second family which played an important role in my life.

Mrs Rajkotwala had come across a dupatta that I had embroidered, and so sent word for me to report to her residence. I was fourteen years at the time and the first thing I recall about that first visit was the distance. My mother and I set off early one morning, we crossed the famous bridge that had stood there for over a century. It was the first time in life that I had ventured onto the other side, and onto the road that led to the shipping port of Mundra. We were lucky to hitch a ride on a cart that took us most of the way, and from there we walked along sandy roads towards the sea.

The house was built by the beach, bordering the Arabian sea. Three sides of the large property were fenced and in it sat a large sprawling colonial house. We entered through an open ornamental gate into a long driveway leading to the house. The house was set among beautiful gardens, trimmed hedges abundant with varieties of pink flowers. Bordering the two side fences on the outside, grew thickets of wild stubbly bushes enclosing the property and giving it privacy. It was called 'Sagar Manzil,' and it was my introduction to wealth and luxury.

The house belonged to a wealthy magnate who had made his fortune in trade and shipping. Mrs Rajkotwala was a short, plump, fair lady who possessed a strong and dynamic personality. Her cotton-wool exterior hid a fist of iron, with which she ran the household with clockwork precision. It was apparent from our first visit that although bossy and demanding, she possessed a heart of gold. Seeing us hot and exhausted at the rear entrance of the residence, to which we had been directed, she gave orders that on all our future visits we were to be ferried back and forth from the bazaar, in one of the many vehicles they owned.

During that, or the many subsequent visits, I never saw the elusive Mr Rajkotwala as he always left early in the mornings for his office in Mundra. However, on one rare occasion, I glimpsed at a tall stately man, with a neatly trimmed beard, as he passed by in a whiff of athar. That is when I learnt that he was the master of the house. Later on in life, when I grew to know him, I found him to be a gentle, kind man who let his wife make all the decisions pertaining to the running of the house and all other family matters. It was some months later that I encountered the two children when they returned from their respective boarding schools for the vacations.

Jameela, the daughter, was two years my junior. She resembled her mother both in appearance and nature and from our very first meeting she took me under her wing. She was appalled when she learnt that I could neither read nor write and made it her mission for that holiday and during all the subsequent vacations, to be my teacher and make me literate. It was after that first meeting that Mrs Rajkotwala requested that I stay over at their residence during the course of the holidays. It was, I think, as much for giving company to her daughter, as to keep Jameela occupied and out of her mothers' hair. Most of the duration of that first holiday I can still recall with mixed emotions. I lived in comfort, sleeping on a mattress in Jameela's room; I had three square meals and was treated very well, but I missed my mother and the lack of independence. I experienced first-hand the sense of treading carefully between two different worlds.

Jameela's brother Hussein, at six, was many years younger. He was a mischievous child who spent much of his holidays playing outdoors. He enjoyed playing pranks on his sister and she indulged him. The only occasion I ever saw her angry with him was once when he addressed me with disrespect. For the most part of that holiday, and the subsequent holidays, I was a rather reluctant student to a bossy and determined Jameela, but over the course of years, I learned to read and write. I also developed a deep loyalty towards the only girl of my age that I could call a friend.

When Jameela turned sixteen, she did not return for the vacation to Mandvi as usual. I missed her presence and company very much, but when she did come back, for a week before her term commenced, I found my friend changed. Her conversation contained mention of people and places that I did not know, she seemed particularly taken up by a young cousin she had met. His name popped up in every other sentence she uttered. It was the first time that I was glad when the day came for her to depart for school.

I was now eighteen years of age and an adult myself. My dear mother was ageing before my eyes. From my early teenage years, I had helped my mother with her sewing, and by now, I had taken over most of her workload, as there were days when her fingers and knees were so stiff that she could hardly get off her bed. I had started venturing out for work on my own but being uncomfortable walking around by myself, for practical rather than religious reasons, I decided to don the burqa. It was a cloak of anonymity, a cloak that kept me relatively safe.

During the following vacation, when Jameela returned, I did not stay at Sagar Manzil. I could not leave my ailing mother and Jameela had invited a couple of her friends to stay. When I did drop in on a visit, I felt thoroughly out of place.

The very next year, I lost my dear mother while my sickly father lingered on. It was the first occasion on which Mrs Rajkotwala had driven up to our shack. She had come to pay her respects and condole with me, but when she observed the situation, she took it upon herself to make a decision on my behalf. The very next morning, she sent her vehicle back with instructions to pack up all my possessions and re-locate to her residence. She and Mr Rajkotwala insisted that I live with them. In fact, they made it out that I would be doing them a great service, as they intended to travel overseas to Colombo later that year. I, too, was adrift at the time, I did not know what the future held for me so I gladly took them up on their kind offer. I continued with my sewing orders but now, my situation and clientele had both changed. Mrs Rajkotwala had introduced me to many of her social circle and so I spent my time undertaking orders which were sent to Sagar Manzil. If ever I did have to venture out to visit a client, Mrs Rajkotwala insisted that arrangements be made to fetch and drop me back in their vehicles.

It was at a charity event hosted by Mrs Rajkotwala, that I was introduced to Mrs Jadeja. I had noticed this lady earlier in the day, not because she was a forceful personality but rather because of her extremely elegant appearance. She was a tall, slim, and stately lady, her silver hair caught up in a low bun. She wore a simple grey cotton saree with just a string of pearls around her neck as adornment. She walked with such grace that she seemed to float along. She stood out because of her simplicity from amongst a crowd of other ladies decked in their rich silk and heavy jewellery. When we were introduced, I was struck by her soft mellow voice and her light grey-green eyes, eyes that matched the rest of her appearance. She requested that I visit her residence on a day convenient, as she wished me to turn out a few outfits for her young daughter. This was the third of the houses in Mandvi that featured in influencing the events that were part of my future.

A week later, Mrs Jadeja sent for me and I entered the third residence that was written in my stars, a house that had a totally different atmosphere from the one I lived in. The Jadejas lived in the town across the famous bridge. Their residence was at the top end of the narrow lanes leading into the bazaar. It was behind a high wall, with an imposing sturdy gate, manned by a gatekeeper. I was allowed in through the main gate only because I was in their vehicle. It was a large rectangular property which housed two separate buildings, connected by a long open veranda. At one end was, as I later found out, the main residential quarters of the family, and at the other was the kitchen and servants' rooms. I was directed to the back section and asked to wait. Unlike the Rajkotwala home, where the kitchens were always a lively and busy place, this place was deathly quiet. I saw a few men scurrying around and felt a sense of apprehension. In one corner of the kitchen, there was an older woman fast asleep, I sat near her and waited.

After a while, I saw Mrs Jadeja approaching down the long corridor, behind her followed a young girl of about fourteen or fifteen years of age, of absolutely startling beauty. She was tall, slender, and fair like her mother, and with the same light eyes, but it was the shape of her eyes that made her appearance so arresting. The upper lids of her eyes were somewhat raised to give her eyes an unusual triangular shape. They were framed by the longest, thickest, black eyelashes I had ever seen. The eyes dominated the pale face. Her skin was like the porcelain of the Japanese figurines displayed in Mrs Rajkotwala's drawing-room, and her long black hair hung loose like a satin sheet up to her waist. She seemed somewhat coltish and awkward next to her graceful mother. She was very quiet and hardly spoke a word. I could not decide at the time if it was shyness or arrogance. She was unlike any young girl I had met, there was something mysterious about her.

Unlike at Sagar Manzil, I never stepped into the main house. I was shown a small room near the kitchen and that is where I spent my time stitching. On my subsequent visits, I did try to draw out some conversation from the young girl but she answered only in monosyllables and mostly remained quiet. For all the wealth and beauty, she cut a very lonely figure.

After a couple of visits to the Jadejas, I did get familiar with the old woman whom I had seen sleeping in the kitchen on my first visit. She loved to gossip, and probably not having many opportunities to do so, and having a captive audience, she enlightened me with all the information that I learnt about this family. Hajara, as was her name, was an orphan, hailing from Pune. She had been employed by Mrs Jadejas' parents as a young girl and had accompanied Mrs Jadeja to Mandvi at the time of her marriage and was completely loyal to her. I got the impression that she disliked the master of the house.

Mrs Jadeja, like Hajara, was born and grew up in Pune. Although prematurely grey and a shadow of herself now, I was made to understand that Mrs Jadeja had been considered a great beauty in her youth. She was one of seven offspring of a government clerical officer. Mr Jadeja had seen her at a wedding he had attended in Pune. She had been one of the friends in attendance to the bride. She had been only seventeen, he, thirteen years older and unmarried. When he had sent in the marriage proposal, her father and the family had seen it as a blessing and she was married off within a few months. She had had no choice. Both Hajara and Mrs Jadeja had never been back to Pune since the marriage.

Mr Jadeja was a powerful man in Mandvi and beyond. Although he did not belong to the more illustrious noble family that carried that name in the state, he was by far the more influential at the time. He owned a fleet of heavy vehicles and controlled the transport of goods, both legal and illegal, from the port of Mundra to the city of Ahmedabad. He was immensely wealthy and could influence most of the politicians in the state. I heard that he was a ruthless man, having a legendary temper. There were many stories, repeated in whispers, of the fate of men who had crossed him.

There were three sons, many years older than the daughter. The oldest Mehul was married and living in the near-by town of Bhuj. The other two boys were both pursuing their studies in England. I had never seen Mr Jadeja as he lived in Ahmedabad, but on one rare occasion when he was in Mandvi and I happened to visit, all I saw was a flurry of vehicles arriving and departing from the main gate. I felt the tension among the staff in the kitchen quarters, everyone in the household, including Mrs Jadeja, seemed to be on edge. The daughter never made an appearance that day.

In fact, that happened to be my last visit there for a while, as the very next week the Rajkotwala family, who had been visiting relatives in Colombo, returned, bringing with them the happy news of Jameela's engagement to her cousin there. The wedding celebrations were to be held in Mandvi the following year, and so began a period of great excitement at Sagar Manzil. Additional rooms were to be built to accommodate the guests, the trousseau prepared, the jewellery ordered, and the food and music to be decided upon. There was so much to be organized that for the next twelve months I had no time to ponder on my future, the course of which had already been set.

# CHAPTER 3

# DEEPANI / 1954 - 1970
# "STILL WATERS."

I should have, as the youngest in the family and the only daughter born many years after three sturdy boys, rightfully been "the pet of the family," " the apple of the eye," but by some quirk of fate, the stars had aligned against me, and an astrologer on whom my father set great store, foretold of malefic influences and misfortune to the males in my family due to me. The result of which was that I was confined to the back rooms of the main house and grew up in the care of my mother, with hardly any contact with my father or brothers. To add to this misfortune, I was also a sickly child and so it was not considered necessary to send me to school to gain an education. I was home-schooled by a local woman who visited daily for a couple of hours. I grew up with no contact with any other children.

My earliest memories of my childhood were playing by myself in the gardens and talking to imaginary friends. This habit, coupled with my extremely pale skin and a face dominated by my unusually light eyes, led most people to consider me an odd and strange child. My brothers, who were very much older, were boarded at a prestigious boys' school near the capital Delhi. I cannot recall any interaction with them, as by the time I had turned five years of age, they had all been sent to Britain for their studies. I knew my father as a stern man to whom I was summoned on rare occasions at a festival or religious ceremony. I cannot remember even one affectionate word or gesture from him towards me. My mother was everything to me. I had heard it from the old maid Hajara that I would not have survived infancy if it had not been for the will and determination of my mother.

To look at my mother now, after four children, one could hardly imagine that once she had been considered 'a great beauty.' She had never fitted into her life in Mandvi, she had nothing in common with the women in that small town and I, her delicate daughter, seemed to be her sole reason for existence. She was my world. She nursed me, protected me, and introduced me to books and reading from a very early age and so, I grew up in this imaginary world of fantasy, a very lonely child.

At the age of twelve, just prior to my attaining age, I had fallen seriously ill. This was a rare occasion during which my mother 'stood her ground' and insisted on having a specialist doctor from Ahmedabad to attend to me. After a great many tests, it was diagnosed as nothing life-threatening, but I was found to be severely anaemic and the doctor insisted that I indulge in some form of physical exercise to strengthen my weak muscles. Sports was not even considered, but my father reluctantly acceded to my mother's insistence and so I was enrolled at an oriental dance academy.

The dance classes were held twice weekly at a nearby school hall. I was always accompanied by the old and faithful Hajara, for whom the opportunity to be gossiping outside the walls of our restrictive household came as a welcome reprieve. For the first time in my life, I discovered an activity I was passionate about, from the very first lesson I loved to dance. I enjoyed the freedom and grace of the movements, I felt I could express myself without words. It was also an outlet for all my pent-up emotions and frustrations and so, as the years went by, I had developed into what my teachers considered an exceptionally talented dancer. It was also the first time I came into contact with other young girls of my age, but maybe because of my status or the reputation of my father, or because I was stiff and awkward around them, they remained aloof, just acquaintances rather than friends. I did not mind that. For me, dance was everything I needed. I poured all my feelings, all my emotions into dance and never developed any close relationships in class.

At fifteen, I had grown to be, what was considered, tall for my age; my body too had developed, making me appear older than others of my age. My mother, realising that I needed new attire, recruited a young girl to visit and sew me some outfits, and so Bhoomi entered my life. Although not many years my senior, there was something about her maturity, her matter-of-fact manner, and her confidence that appealed to me, yet I was so lacking in social niceties that I was too shy to make conversation. In all her visits to our house, she tried to draw me out but, unused to small talk, I clamped up, probably making me appear proud and arrogant... and so the days passed by as usual, till the arrival, one morning, of a 'wedding invitation' by post, that turned my world upside down and changed everything.

The invitation included me, which was the first surprise. It was an invitation to the wedding of the daughter of one of my father's business associates, to be held in Mandvi. Surprisingly, I had been allowed to attend this. For this momentous event in my life, my mother deemed it necessary that my outfits be ordered from Bombay, sandals from Ahmedabad, and the jewellery taken out of vaults and picked to match the outfits. In this respect, too, I was different. Whilst most girls my age would have been excited about the elaborate clothes and jewellery, I was mostly apprehensive. I had occasionally heard it being mentioned that I was beautiful, but maybe due to lack of self-confidence, I myself never believed so. I merely felt that I looked different.

The only activity I was passionate about was dance. I attended every class and it was just about a fortnight before the wedding that I noticed a difference when I walked into my dance class. There was an unusual sense of excitement around, the other girls were all in a flutter, huddled in a corner, giggling amongst themselves. It was then that I noticed the musical instruments laid out, and some unusual faces around. It was rare, if ever, that we had an audience during our lessons, other than one or two occasional spectators who may have accompanied a student to the class. On this occasion, it was particularly unnerving, as all the strangers around were men. Our dance teacher informed us that this troupe of musicians hailed from Karachi, and were here in Mandvi to perform at the forthcoming wedding celebrations. They had kindly offered to provide music for our next few lessons. Most of the musicians were older men, except for the two young drummers.

During that dance lesson, I could not focus as I usually would. I was very conscious of a piercing gaze following my every movement. This particular young drummer was exceptionally handsome. He was tall, had a wonderfully toned physique with golden-hued skin, and long burnished red-gold hair. He possessed the most amazing green eyes and he did not take those eyes off me. When the lesson was drawing to a close, he stopped drumming and, leaving his drum, walked towards me. He stopped right behind me and put his hands on my waist. He then proceeded to hold up my upper arm, as though to indicate that my elbows needed to be higher. His touch did not last for more than a few seconds but I felt as if a bolt of electricity had travelled through my body. I had never experienced such a physical reaction. I was breathless, I felt the blood rushing to my head, my head was literally spinning, I felt dizzy and faint and would have collapsed to the ground had he not scooped me in his arms, holding me close. I knew he felt something too. I could feel his rapid heartbeat, I could see the beads of sweat on his face. He lay me down gently on the floor as everyone rushed to help, bringing water and cushions. I felt him quietly slip away and I resumed breathing.

I could hardly wait for the next dance lesson. I was in a state of feverish anticipation, not quite sure why or what I expected. An unbridled excitement coursed through my body, coupled with nervous apprehension. I could not understand myself, this feeling within me was so unfamiliar. And then, a few days later, there he was again. During this class, he did not join the troupe providing the music. He sat at the back, near the entrance, and though I did not look at him, I felt his burning gaze on me throughout the lesson. When the class was over, I went to retrieve my belongings which were kept outside the hall and, suddenly, I sensed his presence by my side. He did not say a word, he did not need to, the look that passed between us expressed it all. He took my hand and slipped a note into my palm. He turned quickly and left before anyone could notice the encounter. I held onto that note tightly in my hand till I reached home. I rushed into my room and sat on the bed. My hands shook as I unfurled the note. He simply asked if I could meet him in a particular classroom after my next lesson. I read and re-read the note before destroying it. I was both excited and fearful at the thought of meeting him, but the fear did not overcome my determination and desire to keep the tryst. I thought of many an elaborate scheme but eventually resorted to the simplest. I told my mother that my next lesson had been extended by a half-hour or so. She had no reason to doubt my word and so instructed Hajara and the chauffeur, who collected me after the class, about the extended time. Hajara was only too happy to have more time to gossip outside and so it was all arranged.

The troupe was not in attendance on the day I went for my next lesson. I heard they had all gone over to the wedding venue to practice and yet, immediately after my lesson, I slipped away and entered the furthest classroom. He was waiting there for me. This boldness in me was something that I had never experienced, but nothing seemed as important as meeting him alone. He walked towards me and took me by the hand and led me to a hidden alcove at the back of the room. It was late afternoon and not much sunlight filtered in there. He turned towards me and held me in a tight embrace. I lifted my head and his lips met mine. Not a word had passed between us, my heart was pounding and my head spinning, but I did not push him away. I pressed myself closer against him and kissed him right back. I had never felt such a physical response, I was panting, out of breath, and abandoned. I wanted him in ways I never knew about. His hands touched me in places that took me to the heights of ecstasy. He, too, was sweating and moaning, pressing himself closer than ever. I did not understand why but this physical pleasure between us was what I wanted too. I felt him shudder and give a deep groan. The encounter was intense and fast. He pulled away abruptly and sat on a low desk. He sat me down on his lap, stroked my hair, and spoke to me. His voice was like his appearance, it flowed like molten gold.

He said he had fallen deeply in love with me, he said I was the most beautiful girl he had ever seen. He recited verses of enchanting poetry and whispered words of love. He wooed me with his words, he hypnotized me with his eyes and thrilled me with his touch. I was completely under his spell. He made me promise to meet him again, after the next class, in a few day's time. I had no power, no will, and no intention of refusing.

This time I lied boldly to my mother. I said we were having an extra lesson in the following dance class. She did not doubt me at all. I could not wait for the lesson to be over and, as soon as it was done, I slipped out and rushed there to meet him. He was waiting. This time he had prepared a comfortable place at the back, having laid a soft quilt on the floor with a few cushions around. He led me there and gently lay me down. He held me close and rained gentle kisses on my face, whispering words of love. This time it was I who wanted more. I felt the blood rush to my head, my body was on fire; I arched my back and pressed myself close against him. I felt wild, abandoned, my body not my own. I found his lips and kissed him passionately. I heard him moan. I did not resist when he loosened my garments, undoing my skirt and blouse. He touched me in places I had never been touched at, making me moan in anticipation. He hurriedly removed his clothes and rolled on top of me. I did not push him away, I could not. I wanted him as much as he did me. My body ached for fulfilment. I did not resist. When it was all over, he held my pulsating body close, he called me "his own." He said he loved me and he had to take me back with him and I believed him. I would have followed him anywhere. I was truly both physically and mentally possessed. For one such as me, who had lived such a sheltered life, it was surprising that I had no doubt in my mind about risking all that I was familiar with, to follow him into the unknown. That Friday morning, my father returned to Mandvi to attend the wedding. I knew the risk of my flight had increased tenfold but I did not care. Nothing, no one could deter me from being with him forever.

That very same Friday evening was the Mehendi ceremony, and the ladies of the house were invited for it. I dressed for the occasion with great care. My ghagra and choli, with its beautiful dupatta, was from a leading designer in Bombay. It was in a lovely shade of rose. My mother had chosen some old heirloom jewellery to wear with it, this included an unusual pair of diamond-encrusted bracelets which had been designed and made for my paternal grandmother and gifted to my mother at her wedding. Never having done so before, I carefully coloured my lips and used kajal to dramatize my unusual eyes.

I entered the main drawing room that afternoon, following my mother. My oldest brother Mehul had driven his wife down from Bhuj, to join my mother and me, to attend this ceremony. They were seated, having tea with my father when they saw me enter behind my mother. I think the shock they felt at my appearance struck them momentarily dumb. I do not think they ever expected that one day I would no longer be the sickly child they remembered, that one day I would grow up, let alone grow up to be a beauty. The moment when my father recovered from his amazement at my transformation, he sent my brother to fetch his camera. I sensed his mind working out the advantages. Suddenly, I was viewed not as a liability but as an asset. He insisted that my photograph be taken, I knew he would soon be working out an alliance to enhance his position and wealth. I remember my brother asking me to smile, it was the hardest thing I did that day, knowing that soon I would be bringing scandal and shame upon them all.

We reached the venue just as the sun set. The entrance and the road leading to the house were lit up with colourful pandals. The many trees in the large gardens dripped with coloured lights, making the place look like the fantasy lands I had imagined in my childhood. Everything about that night was like a dream, I walked in a daze. I remember people staring as I walked by, not realizing that it was my beauty they were talking about. I remember the troupe playing sweet music from a raised stage in the gardens, but I had eyes only for him. He looked like a prince that night, in his red silk sherwani jacket and his gold tasselled turban. I was mesmerized.

My mother, to her great joy, had met a long-lost childhood friend from Pune. A vivacious lady who had travelled up from Bombay, accompanying a very fashionable young girl. I saw my mother engaged in an animated conversation, reminiscing about old times, and so when the troupe stopped playing during a break in their performance, and he beckoned with his eyes, it was easy to slip away unnoticed. The gardens were vast and crowded, and my mother was distracted. He knew the way, having scouted the area earlier. I followed him as he led me away from the crowds and lights, towards the beach, and then to a thicket of stubbly shrubs. The overhanging branches shielded us from view, we were hidden away in our own private world.

He had prepared a cosy little hideout, somehow managing to procure a thick blanket to lay on the soft sand. We sat down next to each other, I think he just wanted to talk but the moment he put his arm around me, a fire ignited and passion engulfed us both. We lay down embracing tightly, panting with desire. He undressed and lifted up my long skirt. It was a hurried coupling, we just needed to be close. He kissed me passionately before we parted, making arrangements to meet there again, during the next break in their performance. He needed to talk to me about the arrangements he had made.

We left separately, he to get back to his troupe and I to re-join my mother. I found her still engrossed with all the news about her friends in Pune and, surprisingly, she seemed not to have missed my absence. It was the only time in my life that I saw her as she must have been as a young girl: animated, lively, and happy. She was laughing out aloud, her beauty shone through that night. I joined them and sat quietly by her side until we were summoned to dinner. As soon as I had finished, I excused myself and slipped away. This time I found the clearing myself and waited there for him. When he came, he held me close. We sat down with his arm around me, he spoke of the plans he had made to take me with him. We were to leave on the day of the Nikah, just two days from that day. We were to meet at this clearing at the second break of the troupes' performance. He had made arrangements with someone to meet us on the main road and transport us to a spot of rendezvous with the boatman, from where a boat would carry us across the ocean to Karachi, under the cover of darkness. He said everything was in order, he had only to raise the money to pay the boatman. He said he would beg, borrow, or even steal to raise that money. He promised that all would be fine and we would be together forever. He never asked but I saw him glance at my jewellery. I did not hesitate; I immediately removed one bracelet and gave it to him. I did not ask how much money he needed or know how much that bracelet was worth, I did not think of the consequences of the discovery of its loss. I had complete trust in him, he protested but he did not refuse to take it. We parted after a passionate embrace; I could not wait for the moment when we would be together forever.

The missing bracelet went unnoticed and I did not mention its loss, fearing my father's wrath. The next couple of days passed in a blur, but I had no second thoughts, no regrets about my decision to elope with my lover. The only sadness I felt was at the grief I would cause my beloved mother, but the sheer conviction I had, about my future together with my beloved, over-ran every other emotion. I was feverish with excitement on the day of the wedding and my mother, noticing my flushed appearance, considered cancelling my attendance that evening, but I pleaded and promised to rest in bed that afternoon to be able to attend. Again, I dressed with a great deal of care. I wore a grand and elaborate outfit that day, heavily embroidered with pearls and sequins. I wore all the jewellery I had in my possession, I coloured my lips boldly and dramatized my eyes. On that day, I felt and believed that I looked magnificent.

When I made my way with my mother, to join my father and brother, I walked alongside her. I held my head high, my back straight, I did not feel afraid. That day, I was a different me, bold, confident, fearless, and I think everyone noticed it too. That day was the only time in my life when my father acknowledged me with pride, the only time he paid me a compliment, the only time in my life when I felt that I was a part of the family; sadly, it was just when I was planning to tear it apart.

He was not there. The troupe was already performing when we entered, but I did not see him on the raised platform. I melted away into the crowds and wandered away towards the beach. It was easy to get lost in this vast gathering. I never doubted him, I thought he would be waiting for me in the clearing but he was not there. I waited and waited. I went back and forth all evening, checking the stage and the clearing, but he never came. It was nearly ten that night when the guests were beginning to depart and my family too was bidding farewell that it finally hit me. He had not come; he was not there to take me away.

My world collapsed that night. I felt physically sick, I wilted, my new found confidence lost. I cried myself to sleep, deflated, defeated, devastated.

I heard my father leave the house very early the next morning. I picked up the courage to tell my mother about the loss of the bracelet. She assumed that the clasp may have come undone and dispatched my brother to inform Mrs Rajkotwala about the loss. But the subsequent search did not, as I expected, yield any result. My brother and his wife returned to Bhuj that evening. I drifted along like a shadow, taking to my bed and hardly partaking of any food. I refused to attend the dance lessons, pleading weakness. Initially, my mother and Hajara assumed it was a 'bug' I had picked up at the ceremony. Days passed, I was literally pining away. My mother worried and, after a few weeks, when she was insisting on getting the doctor home, I was really sick. I threw up.

# CHAPTER 4

# PAVANI / 1947 - 1970
# "AS THE WIND BLOWS."

"Poor little rich girl" could well have been penned about me. I was born with the proverbial silver spoon, the only child of a wealthy business magnate. I lived in the lap of luxury, I had the best of everything a child could ever wish for, but I had no mother. She had died giving birth to me.

My father, too, was the only child of a middle-class couple, his father had been a bookkeeper in a small firm. From his young days, my father had proved to be a brilliant student but, much against his parents' wishes, instead of continuing with higher studies, as soon as he had completed his tenth grade, he set up his own business of importing textiles. With some astute deals, he started to build up what was soon to be a business empire. His mother, as I was told later in life, was the dominant force in his life, and it was she who was instrumental in arranging his marriage to my mother. My mother was the daughter of the owner of a small textile mill in the suburbs of Delhi which my father was interested in acquiring. She was just out of school and only seventeen years of age at the time of her marriage, my father at twenty-eight was much older, and of a serious disposition.

Throughout my childhood, I had heard the phrase "poor child" whispered among my ayahs, domestic workers, and teachers. Considering my wealthy background, this was an absolute contradiction of fact, but as I grew older, I came to understand what they meant. Apparently, overcome by grief at my mother's demise at childbirth, my father had forbidden any reminder of my mother to be displayed. This must have included me, for in my childhood I rarely, if ever, saw my father. As an infant and toddler, I was in the care of my paternal grandparents who lived in a mansion that my father had built in Bombay. When I had just turned three, my grandparents had both been tragically killed in a traffic accident while returning from a pilgrimage. Probably affected by this double tragedy, following soon after the death of his wife, my father immersed himself in his business, building an impressive empire. He was always travelling and overseeing or acquiring factories and properties around India and overseas.

I grew up in this luxurious and enormous house, served by an army of domestics, had every possible comfort provided, attended the most prestigious school, ferried back and forth in the latest foreign vehicles, but I was so alone. I was about eight years of age when I happened to overhear a conversation between my two old nannies. One remarked that it was a good thing that I resembled my father, and the other agreed to add that it may have been different had I been born a son. This conversation had a profound impact on me. I was a smart and good student academically, but, from then on, I changed into what would be considered a tomboy. I insisted on cropping my hair very short, I threw myself into any sport I could participate in. Physically active, extremely competitive, and academically brilliant, I excelled, winning every cup or prize on offer, but my father did not attend a single event held. I saw him more often featured in the newspapers than in person, as he had, by now, reached celebrity status in business and wealth.

In all the years of my childhood, Bapu was the one person who gave me the love and attention I craved. Bapu had left his family in Madras, at the age of sixteen, to seek his fortune in the big city of Bombay. He had found work as a peon and general help in my father's initial import venture, and continued to work for my father ever since. He had risen in rank throughout the years and was now my father's most trusted personal aide, his chauffeur, his butler, and loyal shadow. Having left his own parents and siblings at a young age, and having no one of his own in Bombay, he was the only one who felt and understood my loneliness. Whenever my father returned home from his travels, Bapu would visit with a gift from my father. It was much later in life that l realized that Bapu had bought them himself. He would attend sports days and prize days if he happened to be in the city, taking great pride in my achievements. He was the only one who sensed my isolation and the only person I was close to.

Mrs Tamara Emmerson came into my life when I turned thirteen. She was the wife of an ex-police officer who had headed the security detail for all of my father's factories and offices. This gentleman had died of a massive heart attack while still in my father's employment. A year after this, his widow took up residence in our house in Bombay. Mrs Emmerson was of Anglo-Indian origin and was around forty years of age at the time. She was an extremely attractive lady, very fair with short bobbed hair and a bubbly easy-going personality. She was supposedly hired as a governess and chaperone for me but she was unlike all the ayahs and nannies I had been in contact with till then.

Things changed with Aunty Tammy's, as she requested I address her, arrival. The most significant change being that my father seemed to frequent the house more often. The large drawing rooms and dining halls were opened up, new curtains and upholstery ordered, furniture rearranged, all changes supervised by Aunty Tammy. My father started entertaining guests at home while Aunty Tammy played hostess. Music and laughter sounded out, chandeliers glistened and lit up the house, wine and spirits flowed abundantly. I heard mutterings of discontent and a sense of disapproval among the old nannies, stiff resistance among the old staff, but nobody crossed Aunty Tammy and survived. She had my father's ear and, surprisingly, Bapu's full support.

Among all the new changes she made, the greatest change she affected was the change in me. From the outset, she set about knocking the tomboy out of me. It was lectures on manners, decorum, and etiquette, and, before long, she had turned me into a proper little lady. My father was a tall, thin man with well-defined sharp facial features, and I looked very much like him. I would have never been considered a beauty but until Aunty Tammy's arrival, I had never given thought to my appearance. She changed all that. She was very fashionable and extremely well-groomed, and she took me under her wing. She took me along to the best hairdressers to style my unruly hair and introduced me to a variety of beauty procedures which she considered essential to be accepted into the social world she, and later I, moved in. Of all the influence she had in my teenage years, the greatest benefit she rendered was awakening in me a great interest in clothes and fashion.

By the age of sixteen, I knew, that although I was not the conventional epitome of beauty, being tall and slender, and with a great posture, I looked good. I carried my clothes well, it helped that Aunty Tammy took me to shop at high-end retail boutiques and renowned designers of the time, and by seventeen, I was considered by those who mattered in society to be a very fashionable young lady. By now, I had long realized that Aunty Tammy was far more than a chaperone to me. She was my father's mistress, and for all the snide remarks, the gossip, and aspersions to her conniving nature that I heard, I admired her single-minded determination to pursue every advantage life had to offer. Although by nature I was quite aloof and not particularly attached to other people, I had grown fond of Aunty Tammy.

When I turned eighteen, I was a poised, well-groomed, and an exceptionally fashionable young girl, and I myself had decided to pursue a career in fashion designing. Enlisting the help of Aunty Tammy, I received my father's permission to leave for London, to follow a course and training in the fashion industry. I loved my life in London. I loved its hustle and bustle, I loved the freedom it gave me to make my own decisions, I loved the independence. I enjoyed the course I was following. I made new friends. I travelled to Paris and Milan and became familiar with the famous brands, and visited renowned fashion houses in Europe. I worked hard, discovering a creative side to me, which I assumed was one trait I had inherited from my mother.

When I had left for London, Aunty Tammy had moved out of the house, and into a bungalow in the suburbs, presumably paid for by my father. I had kept in touch with her, and when I finally graduated with honours, my father surprised me by attending the ceremony accompanied by Aunty Tammy. I think she had a lot to do with it.

I returned to Bombay after four years, armed with my degree, big plans for the future, and full of confidence. Once again, using Aunty Tammy's considerable influence over my father, I set about implementing my own business venture. I had decided to open up my own fashion boutique, carrying my own fashion label, and I had every advantage to set about achieving this goal. My father's factories produced various fabrics I could source.

He owned real estate in the most prestigious locations in the city. With my knowledge, exposure, and intense training in this field, together with the creative flair and some business sense I had probably inherited from my father, I was very confident of the success of this venture. On my return, I immediately set about implementing my plans. Surprisingly, my father did not object and, unlike other parents with daughters of marriageable age, he did not raise that subject. In fact, as unlikely as it was, he seemed quite proud of me.

In a short period of time, I had formed my own company, located a suitable site, commenced renovations, selected suitable fabrics, and started designing outfits to launch my collection. It was a really busy schedule and I was fully occupied, so the idea of dropping it all, to attend a wedding in a remote town called Mandvi did not come as a welcome task. Yet, since I was just building up a closer relationship with my father, when he requested I represent him at the wedding of the daughter of an important business associate, I did not refuse. Mandvi was quite a distance, and as I would be breaking journey along the way, my father had asked Aunty Tammy to accompany me to the wedding. I had met up with Aunty Tammy a couple of times after my return. She was as bubbly and sprightly as ever. I had heard from Bapu that her relationship with my father was a thing of the past, although they remained on friendly terms. I had been considering offering her the position of managing my fashion boutique. She dressed and spoke well, she had always been abreast with the latest trends, and she had the necessary connections to the clientele I sought. This trip together would give me the perfect opportunity to sound out my proposal.

So, early one morning, we set off with loaded baggage, on this long journey together. Having lived all my life in the big cities of Bombay and London, I did not know what to expect from this town called Mandvi, but, when we finally reached, it surpassed all expectations. The little town was a picturesque place, the weather at the time was cool and pleasant, the hosts were warm and hospitable. We settled in comfortably and I was actually very glad I had agreed to deputise for my father.

Then to my amazement, I reaped an unexpected benefit from my visit. My hostess, on hearing from Aunty Tammy of my interest in fashion, invited me to view the trousseau. There, among the many elaborate garments, I discovered the most exquisite hand-embroidered dupattas I had ever seen. In fact, my journey to Mandvi seemed absolutely providential when I heard that the young girl who had embroidered those remarkable dupattas, happened to reside in that very house. Later that day, when my hostess had filled me in on the girl's background, I was introduced to this young girl. There was something about the girl that inspired confidence. The steadfastness of her gaze, her maturity at a young age, apart from her obvious talent, were all factors that prompted me to ask if she would be interested in taking up employment with me and relocating to Bombay. It was a sudden, spur of the moment offer on my part, but it was not a charitable offer of employment. I knew that if I showcased her considerable talent, it would give my label that extra edge to stand out in that competitive field. I knew employing this young girl would benefit my business immensely. I was even more impressed with the girl when she did not immediately accept my offer, even though monetarily it was a good one. She was loyal to her present benefactor and said she needed to get Mrs Rajkotwala's blessing before considering the proposal. A day later, she informed me of her willingness to take up employment with me but she needed some time to complete her present orders and make some personal arrangements. She also needed help in finding suitable lodging in the big city.

Aunty Tammy was in her element in Mandvi. She loved occasions and revelled in the company and, to top it all, she had met an old childhood friend from her hometown in Pune. This elegant lady was married to a local businessman and resided in Mandvi, they had not been in touch for over thirty years. We left after breakfast the morning after the wedding, both of us well-served by our journey out of Bombay. Me, with a girl I had discovered, whose talent I knew would, with the proper marketing, make my label exclusive, and Aunty Tammy with a lucrative offer of employment, the rekindling of an old friendship, and a promise of future visits to beautiful Mandvi.

# CHAPTER 5

# BHOOMI / 1970 - 1978
# "THE GOOD EARTH."

The excitement was over; the marquees, illuminations, and the decorations removed. The guests departed. After receiving the blessings of the Rajkotwalas, I had accepted the offer of employment in Bombay. The Rajkotwala family themselves were soon to leave for Colombo, for the ceremonies there. They intended to be away for a while, I knew the time had come for me to move ahead and forge an independent future for myself. I had been informed that my lodging in Bombay had already been arranged. Mrs Emmerson, the lady who had accompanied Madam Pavani, had kindly offered to house me until I found my feet in the big city.

A fortnight later, the Rajkotwala family left. I completed the sewing orders that I had undertaken and then set about visiting the few relatives and clients I had, to inform them of my impending departure for I knew not when I would return. After my dear mother's demise, and my move to Sagar Manzil, I had only visited my father on rare occasions, to hand over some of my hard-earned money. When I did drop in this time, he was not concerned about my departure but upset about the loss of his revenue. Apart from the Rajkotwala family, the only other family that I cared for and was sad to bid goodbye to was the dear doctor and his good wife, the Amirs, who had been so supportive throughout my childhood. They were happy for the opportunity I had received to better myself and insisted that I write often and keep in contact. Mrs Amir undertook to deliver any money I could transfer to my father. The two sons, my dear playmates, were on their own. Ahamed was a doctor with a practice in Ahmedabad, he was married and a father of two, and Saif, who had plagued my life in days gone by, had moved to Bhuj where he owned a hardware business. The Amirs and the Rajkotwalas were the closest I had to possessing a family. They had provided me with shelter, security, and love, severing these ties was the only regret I felt in leaving Mandvi.

Visiting the Jadejas had not been on my agenda, I had no orders to deliver and had not been to that residence for a while. I had seen Deepani at the wedding ceremonies and, like many others, had been astounded by her beauty. The visit was a sudden impulse on my part as I was passing by the house. I gained entry and found myself once again in this place that had such a dark and forbidding atmosphere. The house was shuttered, a cloak of doom seemed to have descended over it. The gossipy Hajara subdued. I heard from her that the young girl had been unwell for some time and did not leave her bedroom. After a while, Mrs Jadeja did emerge from that room, she was an even paler shadow of her former self. She seemed agitated, distracted, and not particularly interested in my imminent departure. Her query about my lodging in Bombay was purely out of politeness rather than genuine interest or concern, but the moment I mentioned Mrs Emmerson, I noticed a change. She suddenly seemed very interested in the dates and mode of my departure. I never saw Deepani on my visit.

I left, thinking that would be the last time I would be seeing them all. So, I was very surprised when a few days later I was informed that Mrs Jadeja had called over at Sagar Manzil to meet me. The usually calm and sedate Mrs Jadeja was unusually nervous, it took her a while to open up as to the reason she was here, but when she did, she was absolutely direct. It came as a total shock. Deepani's delicate condition, her refusal to disclose the name of the father, her depression, the consequences, all poured out of an agitated mother. She finally pleaded with me to take Deepani along with me to Bombay. Mrs Jadeja said she had confided in her friend Mrs Emmerson, who would meet us there, and that she would make all the arrangements for our journey. Mrs Jadeja did not want anyone to discover the reason for Deepani's disappearance and so the flight was planned to the minutest detail. Hajara was the only other, who was involved in the arrangements.

On the day of my scheduled departure, Hajara was sent to fetch me from Sagar Manzil. We alighted at the top of the lane to the bazaar and made our way on foot to a small shop where we left my baggage to be collected later that night. We then entered a dirty public toilet, where we both donned burqas and thus clad, we gained entrance to the Jadeja residence, where Mrs Jadeja had left instructions to permit us entry. It was around five that evening. As I later found out, the watchman changed his shift at six, so when I left at seven that night with Deepani, now clad in a burqa, we did not raise the slightest suspicion at our exit. Deepani carried no luggage except a small cloth bag, and I just a small sealed package and a letter to be handed to Mrs Emmerson. I collected my luggage from the bazaar and made our way to the main bus stand, still anonymous in our burqas, we boarded the last bus that left that night from Mandvi to Bhuj. Deepani spoke not a word but she made no protest. I had never ever travelled out of Mandvi and was not of a nervous disposition, but this journey to Bhuj was nerve-wracking. Although Mrs Jadeja had assured me that all arrangements had been made, I knew we would reach Bhuj late at night and I did not know what to expect. The streets were deserted when we alighted at the bus station but, within a few minutes, an elderly man hailed us and accompanied us to our next mode of transportation. It was at the back of a long-haul lorry. This lorry was returning to Ahmedabad after unloading goods at the port. I assumed money had changed hands as there were a couple of mattresses, bottles of water, and some biscuits laid out at the back. We struggled up and into the lorry and, in a few minutes, we were on our way.

It was a long and bumpy ride all through that night. We stopped a couple of times to use some rustic facilities.

I was worried about Deepani as she had not eaten a morsel of food. She looked drawn and sick, adding to my stress, but eventually, through sheer exhaustion, I dozed off. When I awoke, it was morning and we had reached the outskirts of the city of Ahmedabad. I was overwhelmed by the hustle and bustle I witnessed around. The lorry finally came to a halt in the city and the elderly man, who had met us in Bhuj, appeared once again. He had accompanied us in the same vehicle. This time, he directed us to a small guest house and after settling us in a room to rest, informed me that he would return that evening to collect us once again. Later that evening, he turned up by rickshaw and transported us to the railway station, where he boarded us on the overnight train to Bombay. The train journey was uneventful, we travelled through the night. I tried to converse with Deepani but she did not respond. We reached Bombay early next morning and, on alighting, I was relieved to hear the shrill voice of Mrs Emmerson accosting us on the platform. It had taken us two days but finally, the arduous and exhausting journey was over. I was in Bombay, at the start of my new life.

We left with Mrs Emmerson in a taxi and, after some time, reached her neat little bungalow, a compact little house, set in a housing estate in the suburbs. Deepani was soon settled into the guest room and I into an adjoining small boxroom. Deepani was now in the capable hands of Mrs Emmerson. I handed the letter and small package I had been entrusted with to Mrs Emmerson and thought that I had discharged my duties and that would be the end of my obligation. I did not dream at the time that it was just the beginning. I settled into my new surroundings and routine, while Deepani hardly left her room. I heard her stifled sobbing every night but she volunteered no conversation other than a quiet yes or no when something was asked from her. A week after we arrived, Mrs Emmerson arranged for a doctor to visit. Deepani was explained away as a niece visiting from Pune. After the doctor's examination, I gathered from Mrs Emmerson that although Deepani was undernourished and depressed, the baby seemed to be healthy and fine.

Madam Pavani had been notified of my arrival. Mrs Emmerson herself had recently commenced work as the manageress of the establishment. A car collected her every morning at eight and she returned around six each evening, bringing with her orders of garments to be embroidered. All the equipment and threads I needed had been provided by Madam Pavani. A young girl Neelam arrived daily to cook and clean, Deepani hardly emerged from her room, I worked hard on the orders undertaken and so began a period of quiet, routine existence. Mrs Emmerson, on the other hand, lived a full and busy life. She had an active social life, she attended poker nights, club nights, dinners and dances and seemed to enjoy them all.

I had visited Madam Pavani's fashion boutique on a few occasions with Mrs Emmerson and, on a day that she was unable to, I undertook to make a delivery myself. On that day, while browsing around, I realized that the garments I embroidered were deemed exclusive and extremely expensive. I was very proud but it made me sad as, unlike before, I did not know the persons who were attired in my creations. I mentioned this to Madam Pavani as she happened to be there that day and hence, she would send for me, to personally meet the client to discuss preferences, particularly if it was for a bridal order. Months passed, I was being well paid for my services. I lived quietly and comfortably, hardly having any expenses except the small sum I dispatched to my father each month, and so, I saved most of my salary. Life was easy but yet I missed the noise of the busy bazaar, the gossiping and bickering of the domestics in the kitchens of Sagar Manzil, and I decided that as soon as I had saved enough I would find a room for myself in the city. Mrs Emmerson had mentioned that after the birth of the baby, Deepani and the child would be taken to Pune to live with her maternal relatives. I felt that would be the right time, to make arrangements to live independently myself.

Deepani's pregnancy and confinement was not an easy one. The doctor was summoned frequently to attend to her throughout the following months. It was late at night when I heard the moans from Deepani's room, it was still a few weeks before the baby was due, but I knew instinctively that the time had come and ran to fetch Mrs Emmerson. Arrangements had already been made with a neighbour, who possessed a vehicle, to transport us, and soon we both accompanied Deepani to the maternity hospital nearby. Deepani laboured through the night, while Mrs Emmerson and I struggled to make ourselves comfortable on the hard wooden benches outside. It was in the morning when we heard a flurry of running feet and loud voices and saw Deepani being hurriedly wheeled into the operating theatre. After a while, when both Mrs Emmerson and I were ready to collapse ourselves, we heard a lusty cry. The doctor summoned Mrs Emmerson while I waited anxiously outside. When Mrs Emmerson finally emerged, she had a baby swaddled in her arms and what a baby she was. A big, bonny girl, extremely fair in complexion, with a thick head of copper-gold curls and large emerald green eyes. Mrs Emmerson walked around holding the baby, saying the word 'magnificent,' 'magnificent' repeatedly. The child looked nothing like her mother, and I could not think of anyone else whom she resembled.

Deepani, as I understood, was being kept under observation as her pressure had dropped dangerously low and she was in a very weak state. I was allowed in to see her and I found her with her eyes closed, her breathing laboured. When I spoke to her, a teardrop rolled down from the corner of her eye. Mrs Emmerson insisted that I return home to rest, while she remained with Deepani and the baby. No sooner than I had bathed and had a meal, a rickshaw pulled up at the door with a man insisting I return immediately. I rushed back to be met by a frantic Mrs Emmerson, there had been complications, and Deepani had breathed her last. She had no will to live, she was no more.

And so, the peace and routine in our lives were shattered. A period of uncertainty and turmoil began. It started with Mrs Emmerson frantically and unsuccessfully trying to contact Mrs Jadeja. I finally made contact with Hajara through the shop at the bazaar to convey the sad news. A few days later, having had no communications from either of them, Mrs Emmerson and I were the only two present at the quiet burial ceremony arranged, to lay Deepani to rest. It was a week later that we got word of the untimely demise of Mrs Jadeja. The relatives from Pune never materialized and so the baby was brought back to the bungalow.

Mrs Emmerson hired a full-time ayah and resigned her post to stay home, while I set off each morning to the boutique and returned at night. Initially, there had been talks of adoption but after a while that died down. Mrs Emmerson, who had been unable to conceive in her youth, had fallen in love with the little one. She adored her. A month after the baby was born, Mrs Emmerson received by registered post a birth certificate. The matron at the maternity hospital had, with all the subsequent chaos which resulted after the birth, taken it upon herself to register the child. She had heard Mrs Emmerson's frequent exclamations of magnificent and thus Magni Emmerson was officially registered and introduced to the world. A year later, using as much influence as money and her former connections to the police force as possible, Mrs Emmerson made it official and formally adopted baby Magni. All the plans I had to move out on my own were shelved as Mrs Emmerson, who had been so kind, pleaded with me to stay on.

Magni was a picture book, beautiful baby who grew up to be a cherubic cute toddler. She was thoroughly spoilt by Mrs Emmerson and everyone else in our neighbourhood. Gone were the days of partying, her life revolved around little Magni. I was the only one who tried to instil some discipline, as I watched her grow into a wilful and stubborn child, and I tried hard to stem her unruly behaviour. I continued to work at the boutique, returning at night to listen to a litany of Magni's escapades from an enraptured Mrs Emmerson and an exasperated ayah. As the years rolled by, Magni was enrolled at school and life settled back into a routine. I once again resolved to move out and live on my own.

Mandvi had retreated to a distant memory. My correspondence with the Rajkotwalas and the Amirs had dwindled to an occasional Eid greeting, so it came as an unexpected jolt when I received a letter from Doctor Amir, informing me of the death of my father. My father, to whom my only connection had been the remittances I sent. It was now almost around eight years since I had left under the cover of darkness, and I made my arrangements to return. It was a long journey back, one I made with some anxiety. The Amirs had kindly invited me to stay and when I arrived, they greeted me with such joy and warmth that I instantly felt I was back home. Dr Amir had retired, now happily occupied with his new hobby, gardening. His dear wife kept equally busy visiting and caring for her grandchildren about whom I heard much. Ahamed was a well-established doctor and his older son, a brilliant student, was well on his way to continuing the family vocation of studying medicine and venturing further afield to Australia. Saif was happily married and was the proud father of four.

My father had already been put to rest. The dilapidated shack, with the land around it, belonged to me and already had an interested buyer. It did not take me long to complete the formalities and complete the transaction. I had a week before I planned to return and, still needing some answers, brought up the subject of Deepani and the Jadejas. Mrs Amir was happy to oblige, she had not known them personally but the disappearance of the young girl had been the greatest mystery and tragedy that Mandvi had ever known. She espoused all the theories that had been floated about at the time, the most obvious being the one of elopement, although with whom it had never been established. The other theory was one of suicide, which was mostly accepted on account of a pair of chappals supposedly belonging to Deepani being found by Hajara on the seashore, although how she got there was not known. The third and the darkest was the theory of murder closely linked to home. This was believed by some due to the sudden death of Mrs Jadeja a few months later. Nobody was quite sure as to the cause of her death but it was widely believed that she pined away and died of grief.

The next day, I hired a rickshaw and made my way to Sagar Manzil. I was not sure if I would find anyone in residence but to my great joy, Mrs Rajkotwala was at home. The house and gardens were as immaculate as I remembered, although the staff had changed. Mrs Rajkotwala was delighted to see me and insisted that I stay for lunch, over which I heard about my dear friend Jameela. She was a mother of two boys with a third due soon. It was lucky indeed that Mrs Rajkotwala happened to be there that day, as she was due to leave for Colombo in a couple of days. Hussein had just completed college and was working with his father in their shipping business. After lunch, Mrs Rajkotwala pulled out albums of her grandchildren and Jameela's wedding album to peruse, and it was while looking at the album that a photograph of the beautiful Deepani with the Jadeja family gave me the opportunity to broach that subject. Here I heard a more restrained account of the mystery, but the story differed in the death of Mrs Jadeja, as Mrs Rajkotwala was quite certain that she had committed suicide.

After taking my leave, I returned, and while alighting at the bazaar, out of curiosity, I was drawn again to the Jadeja residence. The main gates were as usual closed. I peered through the gates at the back. The house was closed and shuttered. There seemed to be no-one in residence, there were no signs of Hajara and having no reason to venture in, I left. I returned to Bombay a few days later, promising the Amirs that I would visit again soon. I left greatly relieved as nobody seemed to have connected my departure to the unsolved mystery of Deepani s disappearance.

# CHAPTER 6

# PAVANI / 1977 - 1982
# "AN ILL WIND."

My business was thriving, my fashion boutique and label had become a household name among the elite circles of Bombay. My business was run by capable staff and I found myself with little to do. I was thirty years old, bored, and restless. One morning, my father collapsed at his office and was rushed to the hospital. Although it was not thought to be anything major, it came as an alarming shock to both of us. I was acutely made aware that although we were not particularly close, he was the only family I had. This incident brought about a change in our relationship. I think my father, too, realized that he would not be around forever and, one evening over dinner, he broached the subject of my marriage. It was a time in my life when I found myself lonely and unfulfilled, so surprisingly I was not averse to finding a partner and companion to share my life with. A trifle past the age of what was at the time considered a suitable marriageable age, and not sporting the conventional ideals of beauty, yet being the heiress I was, I was still considered quite a catch and proposals started rolling in. To be fair to my father, he did not press me or pressurise me, he let me make my own decisions. Initially, all the introductions to potential bridegrooms did not work out successfully. Some I found too conventional, some found me too intimidating, opinionated, or independent. A few were around for obvious financial benefits, and others arrogantly assumed that I needed a man to complete my existence. After many months and many a meeting, when I had almost given up on the idea of marriage, I met someone that I fell madly in love with.

Deepak was the only son of a business associate of my father who hailed from New Delhi. I met him when he accompanied his father to the year-end company party hosted by my father. He had just returned from London where he had been employed. He was tall, handsome, and very charming. He was attentive, yet playful, and did not come on too strong. I was smitten. For the next few months, he wooed me with calls and compliments, flowers, and chocolates. Gifts and candlelit dinners followed all the romantic gestures that I had never experienced. He was a sportsman, he loved going dancing and clubbing, he had a wide circle of friends he hung out with; an extrovert, he was the total opposite of me. I asked him how he had remained single all these years and he openly volunteered information of his involvement with an English girl in London, his parents' disapproval, and how it had proved to be a mistake. I valued his honesty. He was in Bombay to set up a business venture of his own. He pursued me relentlessly and I was greatly flattered to be considered 'special' by him. My father had his reservations, he questioned the fact that with all his education, he still had not established himself in any field. Bapu disliked him, but I would hear no criticism.

Six months after, he proposed in a romantic setting and theatrically on bended knees. I was ecstatic and readily accepted the proposal. We were formally engaged and soon arrangements for the wedding were being discussed. I was not enthusiastic about a grand extravagant ceremony but Deepak insisted that I deserved the best. He revelled in making all the arrangements, he took over the organisation and soon it was heralded as the social event of that year. No money was spared, on the locations, the food, the liquor, and the decorations. His entire family and friends were to be hosted at the best of hotels, the celebrations to be spread over a week. He even accompanied me to pick out my outfits and jewellery and he always chose the most expensive ones, insisting that I deserved the best. I found it endearing. No expense was deemed to be too much, it was much later that I discovered that it was my father who had paid for it all. I did not enjoy my wedding. I found everything ostentatious, even vulgar. I felt I was on display, dripping in diamonds and gold. Deepak loved every minute, from the best of wines and champagne, the caviar, the outfits from the designers of Europe, he revelled in all the attention he got, I was just happy to see him so happy.

Soon after the ceremonies, we left on an extended honeymoon. It was a gift from my father. Deepak wanted to take me to places he had been and wanted me to share in his good memories, and so we left to visit Paris, Monte

Carlo, Zurich, Vienna, Venice, and, of course, London. Paris was all moonlight and roses. I had never liked the taste of liquor, yet Deepak insisted that a drink or two would relax me and so I downed them. I was fashionable, yet my taste was too conventional, too conservative for his liking. He chose clothes which were far more revealing and, although I was not comfortable wearing them, he paid me such fulsome compliments that I donned them to please him. I was so glad to have him, I did everything to keep him happy.

Our first disagreement took place at a casino in Monte Carlo. We had been there every night since we had arrived, and on this night, he was drunk and was losing heavily. With every roll of the dice, he kept getting louder and more boisterous. I was embarrassed, I wanted to leave and tried to reason with him and he turned on me to vent his anger. It was the first time in my life that I had been shouted at, let alone publicly. I cringed as we were politely escorted out. That night he blamed me for his inebriated condition, his behaviour, his humiliation, and his loss. The next morning he was so apologetic, he begged forgiveness, he was so attentive, so loving that I overlooked the incident and convinced myself that it had been just one bad night.

As we proceeded on to Switzerland, Austria, and Italy, Deepak was at his charming best. He loved the bars, nightclubs, and casinos, I wanted to visit the galleries and museums. We visited much of the former and none of the latter. If ever we did go out during the day, it was to shop at the high-end branded stores or dine at world-renowned restaurants. After six weeks of travelling around the continent, we reached London. For a while, before we reached London, Deepak had been making plans to host a large gathering of his friends to introduce me, his wife. He had chosen an exclusive and very expensive restaurant to hold this party and, as soon as we arrived in London, he set about organising this event.

It was in London that I had my eyes opened to Deepak's true nature and we had the first of our big rows. It was over money, my money. A couple of days after our arrival in London, Deepak returned to the hotel in a greatly agitated state. He said he had misplaced his wallet with it all his money and cards in it. He asked me if I could tide him over till he sorted out his finances and his father wired him some money. I had carried a substantial amount in cash and travellers' cheques but with all the shopping, dining, and casinos, that too had dwindled away. I was embarrassed to ask my father for more. Then I remembered that while I was a student here, my father had opened a joint account in my name and his, at a reputed bank, to cover my expenses at the time. I knew I still had some balance in that account since I had never used it after returning back to Bombay. The account was still in operation and so I visited the bank and was extremely surprised at the hefty sum in my account. Deepak was elated. I was rather taken aback when he suggested that, as my husband, his name be included, but this request was politely rebuffed by the manager as my father too needed to be a signatory for the inclusion. Deepak then suggested that we open an account in both our names and transfer a substantial amount to the new one. My father had not got to the position he was at without shrewdness and foresight; Deepak was informed that any transaction over two thousand pounds had to be co-signed by my father. Deepak stormed out but not before he made me withdraw two thousand pounds. He was like a petulant child deprived of a promised treat. He was sullen and withdrawn. He dropped me back at the hotel and disappeared for the rest of the day, with my money.

He returned late that night, intoxicated. He called me names, selfish, penny-pinching, and blamed me for his condition, but it was when he started insulting my father that I reacted and shouted back. He was standing by the bar with yet another drink in his hand, the heavy glass came hurtling towards me with some force, it missed my head and shattered by the bedside lamp. I ran into the bathroom and locked the door. I was frightened, never having being exposed to any form of violence in my life. It was well over an hour when I cautiously emerged to find him sprawled on the couch in a drunken stupor. I could not sleep that night. The next morning, it was a peevish and contrite Deepak, apologizing and begging my forgiveness. He was ever so charming and attentive for the next couple of days. He could not have been any sweeter and I made myself believe that this was the real Deepak I adored, but deep down I knew the honeymoon was over.

After a few days, he needed more money. The remittance from his father did not materialize. I did not want another scene, so I withdrew the money and handed it to him. The only positive result of all this was that the talk of the grand party fettered out. With the money in his hand, his absences were more frequent. I could smell liquor on him when he returned late at night, but I feigned sleep and did not utter a word; I did not want to face a repeat of the prior episode. We were to stay in London for a month, I longed to go home and, surprisingly, after a fortnight Deepak decided to cut short our honeymoon and return to Bombay.

My father was away. We settled in my house which had been grandly refurbished for the wedding. Deepak was in his element there. I was a member of all the prestigious clubs where he entertained lavishly; the bills were all settled by the company. There was a fleet of luxurious vehicles at his disposal. A luxurious residence with its army of domestics, and a well-stocked bar to invite his friends, were to him an entitlement. I played along, the charming hostess, the perfect couple, I was so afraid of losing face. Deepak did not seek work but he worked on me relentlessly, to approach my father for a seat on the board of my father's company. He felt that as the son-in- law, he should be groomed to succeed my father. My business, however successful, did not interest him.

On my father's return, I felt compelled to make the request. My father was not pleased. He spoke to us firmly and directly. He made it very clear that we were to have no expectations in regard to his company, there would be no handing over. This came as a blow to Deepak who had assumed it was a done deal. He ranted and raved in private, but still living under my father's roof, his actions were restrained. Then followed a few weeks of late nights on which Deepak went out clubbing alone, returning intoxicated. This behaviour was reported to my father and, probably in my interest, as a conciliatory gesture, my father offered Deepak a considerable sum of money as a loan to start his own venture. In the months that followed, it became clear that Deepak was no businessman. Every venture seemed to fail, with most of the loaned sum used to sustain his high-end lifestyle. A year later, Deepak had blown all the money. My father did not suffer fools easily and he made it very clear to Deepak that he would not be bailing him out of his failures. When my father left the residence, Deepak threw one of his tantrums and decided that we needed to move to Delhi. He had decided we needed to be alone, he needed to make a fresh start. He promised that he would try harder. I wanted to believe him, I felt I needed to give him a chance to prove himself.

Alone, we were not. We moved in with his parents. The house was not the luxurious mansion I grew up in, I was no snob and would have gladly adjusted to a simpler lifestyle if it was not for his parents. Their days were spent listing out my shortcomings, criticizing every action of mine, and taunting me on my inability to keep their son happy. When I could not handle it any longer, I swallowed my pride and asked my father if he could buy me an apartment in Delhi. I think this was exactly what they had in mind. The demands from them all became more specific. An apartment would not do, it had to be a house, a large house in the best of localities, befitting the status of their son and, eventually, it all came to pass. My only condition was that his parents did not move in with us. It made no difference as they were constantly in the house and Deepak made no objection. What irked Deepak and his parents was that the house had been written in my name, and that became the next bone of contention. Soon after, Deepak insisted that we needed a new vehicle, a foreign car, the latest model and the badgering started once again. They said it would give him status, it would help in his business, that I owed it to him and, eventually, to appease them all, I transferred some money from my business and bought Deepak the car he wanted. Deepak would then resume being his charming self and then it was onto something else. The demands never ceased, a watch he had to have, a diamond necklace his mother liked, another loan for his business, until one day I resisted and refused.

This did not go down well with Deepak. He stormed out of the house, pushing me violently aside. Now started a period of him humiliating me. It started with verbal insults at home and belittling me in public. He was often rude and crude. He started flaunting other women in his company, he returned late at night, intoxicated, some nights he did not return at all. It was after one such night that I confronted him about a woman I heard he was keeping. This led to a massive argument in which I mentioned divorce and he hit me. That night, I moved into a separate bedroom and locked myself in, and thereafter I insisted on maintaining this arrangement. His parents blamed me for their son's behaviour and dissipation. It was I who did not give him the respect he deserved, I who had not provided the adequate funds to keep up his status, I who was too cold, arrogant, and frigid to keep him happy, and the ultimate insult was that I was barren. It all came down to the simple fact that I had not conceived.

The separate lives had other repercussions. Deepak now accused me of having other men. He suspected my every move. He objected to me ever leaving the house. He was slowly isolating me. If ever I asserted myself, he would become aggressive and threaten violence. I had always been an introvert, a loner, and probably due to my insecurities never made friends easily. These years in Delhi had always been spent in the company of his friends, none of whom I was close to. I hardly had contact with anyone at this time. All my life, having achieved success in academics, sports, and business, admitting to myself, let alone others, that my marriage was a failure, was difficult. I endured all humiliation, I lost the confidence I had built up, I was frightened, depressed, tired of the constant bickering and arguments, the mental and sometimes physical abuse; I had given up.

I think the ultimate humiliation was planned, probably instigated by his parents as the only way in which they could get control. One night I found my door lock jammed. I did not think much of it, Deepak was as usual out. I heard him return late that night but he did not go into his room, he entered mine. He was drunk and violent. He forced himself on me. I fought back but he was too strong. He raped me that night and I passed out. When I came to my senses, I was battered and bruised. Deepak was no longer there, I did not know when he had left. I dragged myself to the bathroom, I could hardly walk. I looked at myself in the mirror and it finally registered. I had married a monster and I had to escape.

I do not think they expected me to flee, but I knew I could not face another day. The day was just beginning to dawn, I took the little money I had hidden away, and nothing else, and left the house. I was lucky to find a rickshaw to get to the station, lucky to find a train to Bombay nearly ready to depart. I managed to get on board. I was still in a state of shock, dishevelled, shivering, my only intention was to get away. The train pulled out, it was only then that I started weeping.

# PART TWO

# CHAPTER 7

# MAGNI / 1971 - 1997
# "BURNING THE CANDLE AT BOTH ENDS."

"No, Magni," "Magni no" was the constant reproach I heard throughout my childhood and adolescence. Bhoomi, my ayah, the teachers, the nuns, and my friends all repeated this well-worn refrain, but I soon learnt that the one person who could never say 'no' was my mother. I grew up from being a chubby, boisterous, spoilt toddler, into a wilful, stubborn, undisciplined child, and then turned into a rude and rebellious teenager. I was a rare child who had to be removed from a nursery class as the teachers could not control my aggressive behaviour. I was subsequently expelled from two more schools for indiscipline, defiance, and disrespect. Parents and teachers considered me a bad influence on other students. I could never conform to rules and regulations, I was always ready to argue, and wanted my own way at all times. I did not know why I carried this inlaid anger against authority. In my teenage years, I was an absolute nightmare, but my mother found excuses for all the criticism or complaints that were brought to her notice and, with her around, I felt I could get away with anything. It helped that I was blessed with extraordinary good looks and was accustomed to getting attention from a very young age.

It was at the age of sixteen, when out with my friends one evening, dressed as usual quite provocatively in a short skirt and bright lipstick, that I was approached by a strange man. I probably looked older than my years. He handed me his card, asking me to call him if I was interested in appearing in an advertisement. I had never been a good student, never bothering to apply myself academically, and this offer appealed to me. Much against the wishes of my mother, l made contact and dropped out of school. It was fortunate that the gentleman proved to be a genuine scout and, before long, l was recruited by a reputed agency. I was deemed to be photogenic, my unusual colouring with my burnished copper-hued hair, and startling green eyes helped me stand out in this competitive field, and soon I appeared in a few advertisements in local newspapers and magazines. I also happened to be much taller than the average girls around and was soon offered a couple of modelling assignments. A year later, I was strutting the ramp for renowned designers and had become a much sought out model. As soon as I turned eighteen, I moved out of the suburbs to an apartment in the city, which I shared with two other girls. My career had taken off and so had my outrageous lifestyle. I slept in late most mornings and partied late into the nights, hanging out at the popular bars and nightclubs. I moved with what was known as the party set of Bombay; rich, young boys and girls with too much money, and not much sense. I drank expensive liquor, smoked pot, and partied hard. I had become the hot young model that every rich young playboy in town chased.

My mother had not approved of my living away but she did not try to stop me. In time, she came around to accepting my choice of career, although I think Bhoomi screened and shielded her from much of the gossip around my lifestyle. By the age of twenty, I was a well-established model, much in demand, and was earning good money. There had been a couple of offers for films but I was deemed too tall and skinny for the screen; actors, sportsmen, and businessmen all pursued me. Around this time, my mother fell ill, she had always been diabetic but now she had her first stroke. I hardly dropped in to visit her as I was far too busy having a good time.

It was on my twenty-first birthday that I first ran into him, quite literally. I was out celebrating the occasion with a raucous crowd at a popular bar, and while tipsily vending my way to the restroom, I bumped into him. He was so polite, so gentlemanly, so different from the young men I ran around with. He apologized and left me to join his friends. It was quite a new experience to have a man walk away from me, as I was used to them fawning over and vying for my attention. I was quite drunk and immediately swayed over to his table to invite him and his companions to join in my birthday celebrations. He politely, and tactfully, declined the invitation. This came as quite a shock to me as I had never had an invitation turned down, but barely had the rejection registered when he excused himself and exited the bar with his friends. I did not see him again that night but I could not get him out of my thoughts. I frequented that same bar every evening that I was free, hoping he would be there but it was some months later, and in quite a different setting, that I met him again. It was late one Sunday morning while I was walking the ramp at the prestigious Race Club when I saw him stroll by. I knew that he had recognized me as he tilted his hat and raised the glass in his hand to acknowledge me. I waited anxiously for the show to end. I was used to young men waiting hours on end to meet me, this was the first time I was unsure if he would be around; but there he was, thankfully this time I was cold sober as I desperately wanted to reverse his prior impression of me.

He was absolutely charming, inviting me to join his friends. They were all extremely welcoming and I spent a delightful afternoon, quite different from the usual entertainment I was accustomed to. After the races were over, he offered to drop me home. I was on edge during that return journey, for once, doubtful if he would ask me out again. I contemplated inviting him out but I instinctively sensed that he was not the type of man who would like me being too bold. I was beyond relieved when he asked my permission to call on me again. A couple of days later, I received an invitation to dinner on that Saturday. On the evening of the dinner, he arrived, at the exact time he had mentioned, to pick me up, and so started the most beautiful period of my life.

Rowan Andrew MacLachlan hailed from Scotland and was twenty-nine years old at the time. A tall, broad, large man with a thatch of mahogany hued hair and piercing blue eyes. He was employed at a multinational export company and had been posted in Bombay since just over a year ago. He played rugby and loved to golf. He held old fashioned views on most subjects and valued good manners. He liked reading, particularly on history, and was a rare expatriate who enjoyed learning about India's ancient past and its culture and traditions. He loved living in India. Over time, I learned that he was the second son of a titled family from the very Northern part of Scotland. His father was long deceased and his mother, older brother, and brother's wife resided in an old stone castle. He never flaunted his wealth but I learned that they owned farmlands and distilled their own brand of whiskey. He treated me like a lady. He took me out to dinners at fancy restaurants rather than smoky bars. He taught me to appreciate good food and good wine. He spoke to me as an equal and, more importantly, he listened to my views and valued my opinions. He always picked me up and dropped me back home, he brought the much-needed discipline in my life and grounded me. He treated me with respect. He was the perfect gentleman. It was sometime later that we spent a weekend away together and became a couple. I was, by then, head over heels in love with him. I had had many lovers but he was my first true love.

In the months that followed, he took me along to all the parties and receptions he was invited to, mostly within his expatriate circle. They were all outwardly charming but I sensed underlying disapproval and never really felt included. I stood out among the women like a peacock among a brood of chicken. On most occasions, the men all congregated around us, usually slapping Rowan on the back, their hearty laughter and ribald remarks made me feel uncomfortable. Rowan lived by himself in a company bungalow in an exclusive area in the city. Whenever I did stay over, it was also the other end of the society that viewed our union with displeasure. The local domestic staff were not openly insolent but I felt their collective disapproval. It was when we had been together for nearly a year, and I had become a permanent fixture on his arm, that I felt his friends close ranks. I found that I was not included in most invitations, and when we did run into them around the city, they were polite but cold towards me. They made it clear that I was tolerated but not accepted. I never mentioned my discomfort to Rowan but, eventually, he too realized that something was amiss and decided to set matters straight.

Rowan rented out an apartment in a good residential neighbourhood and moved in with me. The apartment was small and modern. We spent all the time, we could, together. We stopped attending most social gatherings, we relaxed and enjoyed each other's company without being judged. I had changed. It may have been with the sense of permanence, the security of having Rowan living with me. I felt content. I had long dropped out from my circle of wild friends; I liked spending the evenings in my apartment, alone with him. I tried my hand at cooking, to prepare the dishes he enjoyed. I was happy to curl up near him, while he read or listened to classical music. My world revolved around him. I was happy just to be with him playing house.

It was a year after being together that he left for Scotland. I was worried, I fretted, I was impatient for him to return, I missed him so much. He was now a large part of my life, I had never loved or wanted to belong to someone as much as this, and as soon as he returned, I told him so. The following year was like the one before. I was blissfully happy with one difference. As encouraged by Rowan, I reconnected with my mother. I even persuaded him to accompany me to visit her and she adored him. Her health was deteriorating rapidly, so we visited often. She appreciated the great influence she felt he had been on me, and seemed happy, and at peace, that she was leaving me in his care. I lost her a couple of months before his second journey back home. He had supported me through her demise and was now the rock l fully depended on. Having him was the reason I did not feel alone in the world.

I had hoped he would take me with him on his return to Scotland, but he did not think it was the right move. He said he needed to talk to his mother and brother prior to making the introduction. After he returned, there developed a slight strain in our relationship. I wanted to get married, he said he needed time to sort out his affairs back home. His mother had not taken the news of his intentions well. The brother he revered had not approved. I knew he loved me dearly, but Rowan was caught up between two different worlds. It was then that I decided to take matters into hand. I had always been diligent on my intake of contraceptive pills due to the demands of my career, but I stopped taking them. I did not tell him about it. I knew Rowan was a good, decent man, I knew if I got pregnant, he would do the right thing. I tried to force his hand but, much as I hoped, in the months that followed I did not conceive.

Then, one day, a most unexpected disaster struck our lives. Rowan arrived back from his office one afternoon badly shaken and agitated. His beloved brother had been thrown off his horse and was seriously injured. He was needed at home and was to leave that very night. He called me from Scotland some days later to tell me that his brother was still unconscious and he did not know when he would be back.

A long letter followed three weeks later. His brother had succumbed to his injuries and Rowan would not be returning. He had resigned his post here. He was now the laird of his lands and the title-holder, he had responsibilities and a business to take over. He said he loved me dearly, but "duty comes first." He said he would buy the apartment for me, he was sorry he had to end the relationship, he did not want me to live in false hope. He wanted me to forget him and move on. I was devastated. Rowan had been everything to me, my world, my love, my mentor and rock, my support and security. I screamed, I raged, but mostly I just curled up on our bed and cried. I refused assignments, did not step out of the apartment, I hardly ate and, in all my despair, I did not realize that I had missed my menstruating dates. I did not connect the nausea and retching with anything other than this big black cloud that had descended over me. Then, suddenly, one day it dawned on me, I had conceived.

I was elated. I was convinced that once I got word to him, he would be back to take me with him or he would send for me. I tried calling him but the number was discontinued. I wrote him a long desperate letter, pouring out my heart. I waited and waited for a reply, but I never heard back. I wanted to die. I did not want this child. I wanted to sleep and never awake; so, one morning, I closed all the windows and turned on the gas. I do not know how long after they reached me, I cannot remember much except Bhoomi being there. I was rushed to hospital where I remained for a while. I had survived.

When I was discharged, it was Bhoomi who took me back to the house which was now mine. It was Bhoomi who nursed me through the darkest period of my life. If she had looked anything like Rowan, I may have had a different reaction, but when they handed me this tiny bundle, all I saw was a puny little thing, her skin so pale it was translucent. She had jet black hair and the strangest shaped eyes of turquoise. Eyes that dominated her face and did not pull on my heartstrings. I handed the baby over to Bhoomi with the words "she is yours," turned my body away from them and rejected my daughter. To me, she was a reminder of what might have been, the reminder of a time too painful to recall.

# CHAPTER 8

# PAVANI / 1982 - 1999
# "WINDS OF CHANGE."

Back at home, I fell into a deep depression. I felt ashamed and humiliated at the manner of my return. I did not confide in anyone as to the reason I had left. I did not want to see anybody, I did not leave my room. My father left me to grieve alone. Bapu was the only person who, I think, suspected the truth, he sat for hours outside my room without saying a word, and later, tried to console and counsel me. I was not told at the time, but Deepak and his father had arrived in Bombay and tried to convince my father that it had been a small misunderstanding, a minor setback that could be resolved, but my father did not insist I return. About a month later, I was physically sick and the doctor who attended to me at home informed my father that I was with child.

My father visited my room later that day and, after informing me on the doctor's findings, asked me directly if I wished to reconcile. When I refused, he set about getting me released from my marriage as quickly as he could. My father was a shrewd and decisive man. He understood that if word of my pregnancy was made public, he would be held to ransom. I do not know the amount he paid out as a settlement. Subsequently, I heard that it included the house, which had been transferred into Deepak's name, but within six months, at the age of thirty-five, my brief and disastrous marriage was over.

It was after the divorce was granted that I left for the cooler climes of the mountains, accompanied by Bhoomi. My father had rented a lovely little bungalow where we settled in for the duration of my confinement. I was still very frail and depressed but, eventually, with a midwife in attendance, I delivered the only positive result of my short-lived union.

When I returned to Bombay with my son, my distant father turned into a doting grandfather. It must have been a result of the manner in which he was conceived that I did not bond closely with my son. He became my father's prized possession and joy. I hired the best of attendants and nannies to care for him and threw myself back into my business. Genes I had inherited from my father, suppressed and dormant for the past few years, awoke in earnest. New ideas, new plans swirled in my head. My first venture, the exclusive fashion boutique and the designer line was a resounding success. Now I set my sights on a chain of ready-to-wear stores, which were initially only in Bombay, but as they gained popularity, I expanded the stores to other cities as well. As the need to supply stocks to these stores grew, so did my enterprise. I tied up with foreign collaborates and ventured into an ambitious project by opening the first of many garment factories. I was now into mass production and big business. I worked tirelessly, my life wrapped up in meetings, deadlines, balance sheets, and profits. I travelled often and extensively. Over the years, my father had grown to appreciate and respect my business acumen and, in time, he quietly relinquished all his business interests by handing them into my hands. I was now the tycoon.

My son grew up, mostly without my presence in his life. I gave him everything he wanted but my time, but unlike in my childhood, he had the attention of his grandfather. He was the apple of his eye, and for all his absence in my life during my childhood, he made it up to my son.

When I walked out of my marriage, I closed the chapter of my life that was Deepak. I never learnt of the conditions that my father had negotiated regarding the settlement at my divorce, but Deepak never asked or seemed interested in his son. I had occasionally come across photographs of Deepak in magazines, most often with a young aspiring model or actress draped over his arm. He hardly figured in our lives till my son turned twelve when I received a legal notice asking for visitation rights to his son. This move was fuelled, as I was notified, by the result of him once again running through all the money he had been paid as a settlement. Deepak, now in his mid-forties with his once good looks dissipated and calculating the extent of my success and wealth, was once again banking on me to bail him out. I was in no doubt about his sudden interest and intention of getting in touch with his son. I made some quick arrangements and enrolled my son into the most prestigious boys boarding school in the United Kingdom. My father was now in his seventies. He had retired after handing over the reins of the management of his companies to me to administer. He owned a beautiful residence in London and decided to reside there with his trusted companion Bapu, primarily, I think, because he wanted to be close to his beloved grandson.

I did not refuse Deepak visitation rights but I made it difficult for him to see his son. The wheels of legal proceedings moved slowly, and when matters were finally resolved, my son had grown into a proper English schoolboy. He had no interest in meeting his father. He was happy there. He spent his holidays travelling to the continent with his grandfather. He did not miss India, in fact, he was reluctant to return home. On a rare instance when my son happened to be in Bombay, I got word that Deepak was ailing and insisted that my reluctant son visit his father. He was around fifteen-years-old at the time, and it had not been a successful reunion. My son was at a rebellious age and did not like being compelled to visit. I think he harboured a deep resentment towards the absence of his father in his life and, as I was later informed, my son had been totally distant and withdrawn with his father. He never asked or wanted to see his father again, he never did, as about six months later Deepak succumbed to a liver ailment, and all my ties to Deepak were finally cut. The anger I harboured laid to rest.

## CHAPTER 9

# BHOOMI / 1978 - 1999
# "MOTHER EARTH."

I returned from Mandvi once again with the idea of moving out on my own, but this time it was with the intention of buying a small house. I had saved a considerable amount and, together with the money I had made on the sale of the land I had inherited, I felt could raise the capital to do so. I returned to the news and excitement of Madam Pavani's romance and upcoming nuptials. Mrs Emmerson readily informed me on all the details of this very handsome man who had swept Madam Pavani off her feet. I was happy for her but I felt she had changed, and when I did eventually meet him, l was one of the very few he failed to charm; I found him arrogant.

I was inundated with numerous orders that I had to complete for the various clients and outfits for Madam Pavani's own trousseau. I did not have any time to look for a place of my own and, once again, my plans were set aside. Time flew by and soon the great day drew near, but I was not invited to 'the wedding of the year' as it was coined by many a society magazine. The elite of Bombay's business circle, with a host of other celebrities, were at attendance at the various functions. Mrs Emmerson did attend the ceremonies, and so enlightened me with all the details. From the descriptions of the decorations, flowers, food, jewellery, and designer outfits, it seemed that money had not been spared, yet I was mostly disappointed that Madam Pavani had chosen not to wear any of her own creations.

There was another reason why I did not move out. Mrs Emmerson was ailing. She had always been a diabetic, but now she had been diagnosed with very high blood pressure and was unable to get around. She was also dealing with a rebellious and difficult teenager Magni. I owed Mrs Emmerson gratitude not only for the lodging she had provided me for many years but also all the help and confidence she had given, to transform me from a small-time village girl to a smart city-dweller. She had taught me the English language, and not only had she groomed and polished my appearance outwardly but, most importantly, instilled self-belief in my own abilities. She begged me to stay on and I could not let her down.

Although I was not invited to her wedding, a few weeks before her wedding, Madam Pavani had requested to meet me. On that day, she placed a lot of trust in me and appointed me as the manager of her renowned dress boutique. When she returned after the honeymoon, she did not involve herself in the business at all. This was unusual, as Madam Pavani had always been very involved in all aspects of her business. Yet I did not think much of it as I believed that, as a newlywed and having a more active social life, she could not spare the time. I carried on managing the boutique and Madam Pavani made no changes. It was at the end of that year that Madam Pavani unexpectedly informed her staff and me that she would be leaving and relocating to New Delhi. She left her fashion boutique in my hands. I ran it efficiently. Madam Pavani seemed to have severed all ties with her business in Bombay. I now dealt directly with her accountants who reviewed receipts, settled bills, and allocated funds I required for purchases and salaries. I dealt with all the suppliers, orders, and customers. The business was an even greater success, clientele and profits had both increased. I was very proud, sometimes I felt it was all mine. All thoughts of buying my own property had been shelved. Two years had flown by and I had been too busy working.

One evening, I returned after work to find an agitated Mrs Emmerson. Madam Pavani's father had contacted her on a confidential matter and requested a favour. Due to her inability to comply because of her poor health, Mrs Emmerson wanted me to meet him. So, the next morning I called over at Madam Pavani's palatial residence. I could not believe the state in which I found Madam Pavani. This once independent, self-confident lady was a shadow of herself. The physical scars had faded but the emotional scars left behind were painfully evident to me. After a few weeks, as arranged for by her father, I left with Madam Pavani to a mountain retreat, and for the next few months it was not the boutique, but the owner, I nursed and nurtured. Like Deepani, Pavani too was listless at her confinement, not involved or interested in the child she was carrying, but after the delivery of the baby, unlike Deepani, Pavani threw herself back into her business. She had hardened, blanked out the past, and moved on. She was determined to prove herself worthy to the world but mainly, I think, to her own self.

When I returned to Bombay, Mrs Emmerson's health had deteriorated and she was in very poor health. These last few months seemed to have taken a toll on her. Magni was giving her a hard time. Tried as we all might, nobody could control her unruly behaviour. I resumed work at the boutique and was glad to be out of the house. On most evenings, when I returned, it would be to Magni's arguments or tantrums, often before she stormed out of the house to do as she pleased, leaving poor Mrs Emmerson drained and helpless. I could not abandon her too. In the years that followed, Madam Pavani diversified her business and set up a chain of retail shops. Over time she expanded her business and entered into production, setting up garment factories all around India. She was emerging as a young and dynamic business entity herself.

Magni, meanwhile, quit school at sixteen and found her niche in the world of modelling. She first appeared in newspapers and magazines but was soon walking the ramp at prestigious fashion shows. She earned good money and, as soon as she turned eighteen, moved out to live on her own in the city. I read of her wild ways in various gossip columns and magazines which I carefully kept out of Mrs Emmerson's hands. Mrs Emmerson was slowly sinking but her beloved Magni hardly found the time to visit, until she met Rowan.

Rowan was, as I and everyone else who knew Magni believed, a very good influence on her. As time passed, we could all see the change in her lifestyle. She was still a top model in the industry but she no longer made scandalous headlines. Then, one fine day, a couple of years after we had heard of him, Magni brought him over to introduce him to her mother and me. Mrs Emmerson thoroughly approved, in fact, after a few more appearances in our lives, she grew to adore him. She was in her seventies now and after nearly two decades of turbulence, she finally found peace in her later years, as she believed she was leaving her beloved Magni in good hands.

A few months prior to her passing, Mrs Emmerson had entrusted me with two items for safekeeping. One was her last will in which she left the house to Magni, and the second was the package which I recognized as the one I had carried with me from Mandvi many years ago. It was still in its original packaging, but when she opened it up to show me the contents, a number of glittering jewellery items spilt out. It was only then that I realized the value of the package I had carried with me. Among all the golden necklaces, bangles, and rings, was an unusual piece that caught my eye. It was a unique and intricately fashioned, unusual gold bracelet, studded with diamonds. After viewing all the pieces, Mrs Emmerson carefully repackaged it and instructed me to give it to Magni on the day of her marriage.

Early one morning Mrs Emmerson suffered another stroke and, on that very day, succumbed to the disease that had plagued her for many years. With the passing of Mrs Emmerson, and Magni settled in an apartment in the city with Rowan, there came a period of quiet, calm routine in my life. I continued living in the bungalow along with the young girl Neelam, who had stuck by Mrs Emmerson and me through the years. She was married and, along with her husband, took care of the house.

The peace was shattered many months later, on a Sunday morning, when luckily I happened to be home. It was around nine that morning when I received a frantic telephone call from the owner of the apartment adjoining Magni's. She was worried as there was a strong smell of gas emanating from the apartment and there seemed to be no occupants. She and I both assumed that Magni was out on an assignment and had left a gas ring on. I rushed over with the spare key which was in my possession. We did not expect to find Magni there. I had not seen Magni for quite a while; I did not know the situation and I was shocked to find her in that condition. We rushed her to the nearest hospital; We had been in the nick of time as she was still alive. It was in the hospital, while she was still under observation, that I learned of her pregnancy.

When Magni was discharged from the hospital, I brought her back to her own bungalow and for the third time in my life, I nurtured an expectant mother. I returned to that apartment some weeks later, packed up all her belongings, and returned the keys to the owner. Magni was back home. She never confided in me, I never knew what led her to take that drastic decision, she did not trouble me in any way during the months that followed, she did not venture out and hardly spoke a word.

When Deepani was with child many moons ago, I was very young myself, with dreams of love, marriage, and children. During the time of Pavani's pregnancy, I still had hopes of finding a companion and starting a family. Now, on this occasion, I knew love, marriage, and my dreams of having children had all passed by me, so when Magni handed this little, helpless baby to me with the words "She is yours," a powerful and maternal emotion awoke in me.

Magni left the house as soon as she had recovered after the delivery. She did not look back. I do not know where she went but she soon resumed her modelling career and, with it, her former notorious lifestyle. I constantly saw photographs of her in various tabloids and gossip magazines but she never called or returned to visit. Her tragic life was cut short when her baby turned two years old. I heard about it initially on the news. Magni had been returning after a party, late at night; she had been driving at high speed and crashed into a concrete post and died instantaneously. It was later revealed that she had been intoxicated at the time.

It was some weeks later, after I had completed her funeral rites and was back working at the boutique, that I happened to hear two ladies talking of the tragic death of Magni. One of these ladies mentioned that at that party, an expatriate lady, a former acquaintance of Rowan, had informed Magni that Rowan had just been married.

# CHAPTER 10

# PAVANI / 1999 - 2009
# "SECOND WIND."

W hen I closed the chapter in my life that was best forgotten, I opened another, and the success and accolades that came with it was immensely gratifying; but it came with consequences. There was a distance in miles as well as emotional connection between me and my only son. My son had inherited his father's handsome looks, he excelled academically like me and was shrewd and ambitious in nature like his maternal grandfather. He was very British by upbringing, a somewhat cold, distant, and reserved young man.

My father died peacefully in his sleep a few years later, at the age of eighty-five, and my son inherited large sums of money and many valuable properties that made him an extremely wealthy man. I inherited his company and a mystery to resolve. All my life I had carried this guilt of having caused the death of my mother and my father's enormous grief, so the discovery of the document came as a great shock. While sifting through the papers locked in his safe at home, along with a large box of jewellery presumably belonging to my mother, I found an old faded certificate, granting my parents a divorce. It was dated nearly a year after my birth. The shock, hurt, and anger I felt at that moment was almost physical. Initially, after I had recovered from the pain, I decided to let go of the past and forget that the document existed, but it wasn't to be. I could not let the matter rest. There was just one person I knew who could provide me with the answers. So, the very next day, I took a flight to Chennai. Bapu had retired and returned to his native village. He had been with my father as a loyal employee from his youth and was now a relatively wealthy man. He too was old now, but he was the only person who could unravel this mystery and enlighten me. Bapu was happy to see me but reluctant to divulge any information regarding the past. But with the help of some tears and a persuasive argument that my father was no longer alive, I coaxed the story out of him. What was surprising was that, although he had been ever so loyal to my father throughout his life, Bapu was sympathetic in his narration towards my mother.

It had been a marriage arranged by my grandmother. My mother was the only child of an associate of my father and the owner of a business my father wished to acquire. She had just completed her schooling and was a pretty, fun-loving, bubbly young girl who loved shopping, dancing, and parties. My father had been many years older and of a serious disposition. He had just been building up his business, always tied up with his work and with no time to spare to spend with his young wife. My grandmother, her mother in law, had been the dominant force in the house. She had been very strict and held conventional views on the role of a daughter-in-law, and between her and my father, they had managed to subdue my mother's lively spirit. She had been desperately unhappy and, within six months of her marriage, already pregnant as expected.

According to Bapu, she had met a young American attache at a rare embassy party my father had been compelled to attend, to which my mother accompanied him. This young man had been placed next to my mother at the dinner table and had sensed her sadness and loneliness. He paid special attention to her. Their relationship had started as a friendship, they met at the club where they were both members and he had been a sympathetic ear, but soon deeper feelings developed between them. He had made all the arrangements and, a little over a month after she delivered me, on a day my father was out of town, she left me and a letter, and walked away. By the time my father returned, my mother and her new love had already departed to the United States of America. My father and grandmother had buried all traces of my mother's existence, with the only exception being myself. I, who had walked out of an unhappy union myself, should have understood, but it was hard to accept and forget that she had not only rejected her husband but had abandoned me as well.

I returned to Mumbai. I had a name and with all my contacts at the embassies, it was not difficult to trace an address. I discreetly hired a private investigator and, to my amazement, I soon found details of my mother very much alive and living in New York, along with her husband and my step-siblings, twins born ten years after me.

My father's death had also compelled my young son to return rather reluctantly to Mumbai. Having inherited great wealth, he was now among the most eligible young men in India. My son found life back in Mumbai different and difficult. He hated the crowd, the traffic, and the dust in this city. After a brief visit to the capital, he decided that he preferred living in New Delhi. He also decided to branch out on a different business path and ventured into the world of advertising and marketing. With that, he founded and ran his own advertising and modelling agency. As he too climbed up the corporate ladder and achieved success, I could not help but read of his playboy image in various magazines and gossip columns. He, like his father before him, was always featured escorting beautiful young girls, and I feared the genes he may have inherited.

It was during a time when I was contemplating my own retirement, a time of reflection and a realization that I was not close to my only son, that I set about trying to establish a better relationship with him. We both knew that this large business empire was his to run in the future, and so I asked and he agreed to accompany me to visit the various factories and enterprises we owned. It took many months, we travelled to all parts of India and abroad to meet business associates and clients. He learned the fine art of balancing the retail and production lines of my business from me, and although we never grew as close a relationship as I had hoped, I think he started to respect me and I started to understand him.

It was nearly four years since my father passed. I was over sixty years and had grown tired of the daily grind and stress associated with big business; it was also four years since I had learned of my mother's existence. Much as I had tried to suppress the desire, I had always had this deep yearning to seek out my mother and, in some way, the time spent with my son had made me understand her decision to leave me and tread her own path. I had come to realize that I had done the same.

I knew my mother was ageing, I knew that I may be running out of time, so I came to a decision and decided to reach out to her. I tracked down the contact number of my step-sibling and called her. I did not know what her response would be, but I was absolutely unprepared for her joyful reaction. She was delighted and so we made plans to meet. I had not spoken about the existence of my mother to anyone and most people around assumed that I was taking a well-earned holiday after my retirement. I flew to New York, and the day I met both my step-siblings could not have been happier. There was no awkwardness, it was a spontaneous and natural connection, we bonded. I, who had been the only and a lonely child, for the first time in my life, felt a sense of belonging; I was comfortable and relaxed in their company. I was surprised at how much they knew of me, for although I had been unaware of their existence, my mother, I heard, had followed my life with avid interest.

It was soon to be my mother's birthday and my siblings had planned a small gathering of close friends and relatives at her house, they wished me to attend and arrive sometime before her other guests. I was excited yet nervous and apprehensive not only about her reaction but also of my response. I did not know what I should expect, but I need not have worried as the recognition was instantaneous, there was no need for introductions. When I entered with my siblings, she took one look at me and burst into tears, tears of joy.

In the days that followed, it was revealed that when she left my father, she had also been disowned by her own parents and she had made them a promise never to step foot into India, or ever make contact with anyone in the family. I also found out that although she could not contact me personally, she had dozens of albums and scrapbooks documenting my life. She had received the photographs anonymously, but she had always believed it was Bapu who sent them; and every newspaper article and magazine cutting she could get her hands on, she had collected from the Indian community in New York. My childhood, my graduation, my wedding, my accomplishments, achievements and awards were carefully compiled. It came as a surprise that my mother had made me a part of her life, although I had never been aware of her existence.

I finally met and got to know the man who had taken her away from me, and I understood exactly why she had left with him. He had risked everything and ruined his career for my mother. I knew it must have been hard on him, in those times, to gain acceptance, but even after six decades, I could see the love and respect they had for each other. It was something she may have never known if she had remained in India with my father. For the first time in my life, I felt loved and wanted, a part of a family. I felt I had come home.

# CHAPTER 11

# BHOOMI / 2012
# "SCORCHED EARTH."

A sharp shooting pain, a visit to the clinic, all was not well. It had spread; six months, a year, who could say, it is as God wills.

She had grown up, this beautiful young girl of mine. My daughter, my life. She was just fifteen, already much taller than the other girls of her group, long limbs, long torso, and long lustrous jet-black hair. She was fair of complexion, with pale translucent flawless skin, skin you would compare to porcelain, but what really stood out were the startling blue-green eyes. Eyes that reminded Bhoomi of the girl's grandmother, not because of their colour but their unusual shape. Eyes that dominated her delicate face, eyes that mesmerized everyone.

I was worried. Although she had not, I had noticed a few lustful eyes following her graceful walk back from school. She was so innocent, this beautiful daughter of mine. Unlike her mother, she had not given me a moment's trouble; a good student, a good girl whose only passion, as yet, was dance. I knew I had to make arrangements to keep her safe, she was still so young.

My old benefactors Mr and Mrs Rajkotwala had passed on. The good doctor and his wife were no more.

I wrote to my good friend Jameela and then, hearing that she was back in Mumbai from her frequent sojourns abroad, I decided to visit Madam Pavani. I had long retired from my employment to be at home with my daughter. I received a generous pension but I had hardly ever seen Madam Pavani since the time of my retirement. I called over at the residence and she was delighted to see me. Madam Pavani seemed a much happier person now. When she heard about my illness, she first offered to pay for any treatment I required, but when she understood that there was nothing more to be done, she promised me to undertake the only request I had ever made of her. She assured me that she would speak to her lawyers immediately and make my daughter her ward when I was no more. She laid all my fears to rest and, true to her word, a few weeks later, I was contacted by the lawyers and signed the necessary papers, leaving my beloved daughter in her care after I had passed on.

My friend Jameela did not reply to the letter, she flew over to Mumbai to see me. She arrived at the bungalow and she, too, offered all assistance to find the best of medical care for me. My dear friend was as bossy and maternal as she had been in her youth, but she too understood that my time was drawing to a close. She met my dear daughter at the time, and she offered me an assurance that she would look out for her wellbeing in the future.

Nearly a year went by, and I knew my end was near. I made the necessary arrangements and spoke to my dearest daughter about the role Madam Pavani would take in her future. I wrote a long letter to my child explaining my part in the past. I felt she was still too young to comprehend it all, so I left the letter and the deeds of the house with the lawyers with the instructions that they be handed over on or after her twenty-first birthday. I left the valuable package of jewellery in Madam Pavani's care, to be given to my child on her eighteenth birthday. I was tired and worn out physically, but at peace; I was certain I had made sure my daughter would be in good hands once I was no more.

My life had held many surprises. I had seen my life progress beyond my childhood expectations, I had achieved success. God had been kind to me, but the greatest gift he bestowed on me was the joy I experienced in the last fifteen years of my life, with the gift of the love I had, from my most precious, wonderful, loving daughter- Surya Chandni Taare.

# CHAPTER 12

# PAVANI / 2009 - 2012
# "TAIL WIND."

Upon my return, after the excitement of my being reunited with my mother, I was bored. Retirement did not suit me. I had never liked attending social events and had always been one to help with charity by donating cold cash. I was once again restless and lonely. My new relationship with my mother had brought about the realization that although my mother had abandoned me physically, she had learnt more about me from a distance than I ever knew about my son. I felt I needed to remedy this situation and decided that I would make it my priority to get to know him and understand him as a person and not just as my business successor. As a first step, I started spending far more of my time in New Delhi.

I visited his offices often and usually went unannounced. I observed him at work and tried to get him to lunch or dine with me. I discreetly inquired about him from people who he employed or socialized with. I found, on a positive note, that my son was brilliant in whatever work he undertook. He ran his business efficiently and successfully, yet I discovered that as a person he was more feared than liked. He was known to be cold, detached, and even ruthless by nature. My son worked alongside some of the most beautiful women in India, actresses who featured in the advertisements he produced and the top models that were part of his agency. He was often featured on television and magazines, in the company of these young actresses and models, yet it seemed he did not sustain any relationship for long. I even spoke to a couple of the girls who he had dated and had them label him as 'a cold fish.' I understood, for as much as I tried, it was difficult to bridge the distance between us.

Among all the various companies and businesses he had inherited and owned, he personally managed 'The Agency,' which was his passion. Here, I also found, lay his obsession. My son, I learnt, had been on a mission for the last couple of years to find that one person who he felt would represent the modern face of India. A face that could be marketed internationally, a face that could launch a thousand products and campaigns. This obsession of his had him looking through hundreds of photographs and video clips and, as gorgeous as most of the girls were, he had been unsuccessful in finding that singular face, his signature supermodel, who could represent his agency and him.

It was around this time of my life when on my return to Mumbai, I was visited by my old protégée Bhoomi. She was the one who had created my signature apparel and seen me through the most difficult period of life, and to whom I was eternally grateful. I was surprised but delighted to see her, but I soon learnt that this was not a social call. Bhoomi was ailing, it was terminal, and she had just one request. I owed Bhoomi a debt, I now had a chance of repaying. I agreed to foster her daughter once Bhoomi was no more. I knew of the girl that Bhoomi had adopted, she had been the reason Bhoomi had retired from my employment, I had never seen her. The girl was young, a teenager; my parenting skills were questionable and I did not know what I had agreed to undertake, but I would not, and could not, refuse Bhoomi the only thing she had ever asked of me.

About a year later, I got the call that Bhoomi had breathed her last and painful breath. I was overseas at the time and made arrangements to return immediately. The very next day after my return, I made my way to the old familiar bungalow of Aunty Tammy. The funeral, as per Bhoomi's faith, was already over, but it was the daughter I had to meet.

As soon as she opened the door, the moment I saw her, I knew. Here, in its raw, unpolished state was the girl my son had been in pursuit of for so long. I saw the unrefined product and I already sensed the potential. Here lay the project that would occupy my restless days of retirement. She was beauty personified, all the more endearing as she was totally unaware of it. She needed exposure and polish. Here lay the means to connect with my son, I had found my bridge.

# PART THREE

# CHAPTER 13

# SURYA CHANDNI TAARE /
# 2012 - 2017
# "RISE AND SHINE."

The first fourteen years of my life passed with unremarkable incidents and remarkable smoothness. It was routine, peaceful, and secure. Although I was an orphan, my grandmother gave me all the love and care needed to make up for the loss of my parents. I did not remember either of them, it had always been my Ummi as I called her, in my life. It was just after my fifteenth birthday that I knew my beloved Ummi was very ill, it was also at the end of my fifteenth year that I lost her. It had been a year of sorrow, a year she tried to face bravely through all the pain, a year to mourn, and nothing prepared me for the year to follow. After the devastation of losing the one I loved most in this world, the rock I had depended on, my life as I had known, changed.

Ummi had placed me in the care of Aunty Pavani, a lady I had heard much about but never met. She arrived a few days after Ummi's funeral, an elegant lady who took immediate charge. In a very short while, as I found out, she had made definite plans for my future. I, who was alone, a minor and quite adrift, had absolutely no choice. She made all the arrangements. The house which was in my name was left in the care of the ever-faithful Neelam and her husband. I had just completed my tenth standard and wished to study further and I would, but never in my wildest imagination had I thought it would be in the United States of America. Within a month, I was on a flight with Aunty Pavani, already enrolled at a prestigious high school in the state of New York.

It was a residential girl's school, and it was surprising how soon I adjusted and settled into life there. I was very lucky as my roommates were two wonderful American girls who made me feel so welcome and helped me settle in comfortably. I enjoyed my time at school and the vacations I spent with this delightful old couple whom Aunty Pavani knew, and who were so very kind towards me. The eighteen months in high school sped by, I had not been back to India since I left, and I was in no hurry to head back. I loved living in New York and wished to enter college there. I was busy in the process of applying for grants and scholarships when Aunty Pavani visited and informed me that she had other plans for me. She had enrolled me in a small but very prestigious finishing school. It was not what I had hoped to do or study, but it was the career she had chosen for me. I knew that although she was my guardian, she need not have taken such a personal interest in my future and, as such, I was grateful and reluctant to protest or object to her decision. It was an unexpected, new, and daunting experience. My mentor was a very tough little French lady in her fifties and, for six months, she drilled me as hard as any army sergeant. While studying proper etiquette in every conceivable situation, I was taught how to hold my posture, sit, stand, walk, and pose. During the next six months, Aunty Pavani insisted I apprentice at a small but elite modelling agency where the tilt of my head, the thrust of my hip, and my walk was perfected till, eventually, I was felt to be ready to walk the ramp. It was initially for small private audiences but, as I built up confidence, I started rousing the interest of the bigger agencies and had offers to model for well-known design houses in New York.

Aunty Pavani had other ideas. She had decided it was time for me to return to India. Although my time in America had broadened my outlook in life, and I presented a polished, confident outward appearance, being quite alone in the world had me inwardly still insecure. I felt beholden to Aunty Pavani for all she had done and so I did as I was told. When I returned to India, along with a fashionable wardrobe, it was a different me. Heads turned when I walked past, I wondered what Ummi would have made of the new 'me.' I returned to a joyous reception from Neelam and was somewhat relieved to be back. I knew Aunty Pavani had undertaken to overlook my finances till I reached the age of twenty-one, but I thought I could now start to stand on my own feet and look for employment in Mumbai. Here again, I found Aunty Pavani had other plans. She requested that I accompany her to New Delhi.

Before we left for New Delhi, Aunty Pavani presented me with a package which she explained had been left to me by my beloved Ummi. When I opened it up, I could not believe my eyes, it contained some pieces of exquisite jewellery. Ummi had been the simplest of souls and I wondered how she came to possess such valuable items. I could only surmise that these precious items had been owned by my mother.

It was in Delhi that I met Lohan. Aunty Pavani took me along to visit her son. I knew Aunty Pavani had a son, and he being one of the wealthiest and most eligible bachelors in India at the time, I had read many a report of him, both in business and gossip columns of various newspapers and magazines. He was expecting a visit from his mother, but I do not think he was expecting me. Lohan was a very handsome man in his thirties, he was a suave, well assured, polished, articulate, but at our first meeting, he seemed to be at a loss of words. He did not speak to me but I saw him observing me like an exhibit. When Aunty Pavani eventually introduced me, something did not feel quite right, it was as if she was making an offering.

Here was where I got my employment offer. It was a very good one and one Aunty Pavani insisted I accept. Lohan had approved and here was where, about a month or so later, I was professionally launched at the Indian Fashion Week, the new face of The Agency, the face of modern India. As a model, I was an instant hit, 'a showstopper,' professionally successful, financially independent; but knowing no one in this city, I was very much on my own. Initially, Lohan treated me like an expensive and exclusive commodity, but as the months went by and I started acquiring a following, I noticed a change. I was now featured on many covers, appeared frequently on television, speculated about on social media, and had become a celebrity of sorts. With my growing popularity, Lohan started treating me as a possession. It was a gradual shift in his manner towards me, but it became very clear on one particular night when I appeared as a showstopper at an event attended by some celebrities. At the after-party that followed the event, a young and popular cricketer kept flirting with me. I was amused and flattered at his persistence. I saw Lohan's reaction, I sensed his displeasure, but I felt it was directed at me, rather than the young boy. He made sure that I made an early exit, but his behaviour that night made me uncomfortable and was the forewarning of what was to follow.

It was after that night, I noticed Lohan had started monitoring my movements; everything I did was reported back to him and every decision I made regarding assignments and invitations had to have his approval. My life in New Delhi was quite routine as I did not have friends in that city, but when I visited Mumbai, he frowned upon any interaction or communication I had with my old classmates or neighbours. Gradually, it became apparent that he influenced and decided every aspect of my life. The assignments and contracts were his business, but interference in my personal life was quite disturbing. Lohan had started escorting me everywhere. He made no physical advances and showed no emotional attachment other than anger or displeasure if I displayed any signs of independence. I was slowly being isolated, it was as if I was a prized possession. I do not know why I did not object, but I was still young, insecure, feeling obligated, and still a ward of his mother till I turned twenty-one years. My career, my income, my success, and all the trappings that it included was tied up in this bizarre arrangement; it was easier to go along.

It was sometime later that I witnessed the darker side of his nature. I had heard stories, gossip among the models I worked with, regarding his relationships and his dismal treatment of some of them, but I had never thought much of it at the time. My eyes were opened when I experienced it. A young upcoming movie star had become besotted over me. He attended every event in which I featured, sent me bouquets of roses, and hung around me at parties if I happened to be there. He was handsome, charming, and persistent. After speaking to him at a few of the social events, I found him to be an amusing and likeable person, I enjoyed his company and attention, and agreed to meet him privately. I managed to elude Lohan and met up with the young man one evening. He wined and dined me at an exclusive club and it was inevitable that we were spotted and photographed together, about which we were both unaware. A few days later, a furious Lohan stormed in at the rehearsal of a show I was preparing for, he berated me loudly for embarrassing him, threatened consequences, and forbade me from seeing the young man again. It did not seem to matter to Lohan that there were others around, he seemed unhinged and, for the first time, I felt fear. I knew this was not normal behaviour, and it struck me that Lohan regarded me as his own property, and it was then that I realized I needed to get away.

I would never have considered entering the pageant before this incident, although many in the industry had made the suggestion. I had usually laughed it off, but now I saw it as a way to distance myself, as a means of escape, and so I sent in my application. I was not sure as to how Lohan would react, I was still under the contract of The Agency, but when he learnt that I had been selected as a contestant, he was surprisingly supportive. I think he liked the idea of me winning that title, and the prestige and fame that came with it mattered to him. He was involved in all aspects of my preparation. He hired a team of experts to help me win this competition. He made sure the training was so intense and hectic that I had no time or inclination to form any lasting relationships outside of work.

I won that crown at the pageant, I was chosen 'Femina Miss India,' and became even more of a celebrity, but it did not, as I had expected, bring me much respite from Lohan. He escorted me to every event, he accompanied me and prepped me for every interview. He made sure he featured in most of the photographs taken and that every article carried our names as a couple. It was a good ploy as, although I was single, it kept any man with any interest in me at bay.

The respite arrived some months later and unexpectedly. As the reigning Miss India, I had to represent the country in the forthcoming 'Miss World' pageant, and the holders of that franchise had their own team of consultants and organizers who were allocated for my preparation and participation. Thankfully, Lohan had little influence and no control there. He was livid and he distanced himself from this contest. He probably did not have much expectations and did not want to be associated with any result that did not guarantee success. Later that year, I left to participate in the contest. Lohan did not accompany me, I was on my own, away from Lohan's obsessive hold, free.

# CHAPTER 14

# SURYA CHANDNI TAARE / 2017
# "BLAZING STAR."

I arrived back in India and to a rapturous reception. Both Lohan and Aunty Pavani were at hand to greet me. I think I had exceeded both their expectations. The month that followed was both physically and emotionally draining. Physically it was a hectic round of felicitations, interviews, talk shows, and parties, which I was obligated to attend. On every occasion I appeared in public, I was groomed to perfection, smiling, looking gracious and radiant, no one realized the emotional turmoil I was undergoing. From the moment I returned, Lohan had been impossible to handle. He shadowed my every movement, looming physically behind me at any public event. He tried to dictate my every move, he had become even more obsessive and controlling. Yet, what worried me more was that he seemed to want commitment to a deeper relationship. He made me very uncomfortable and frightened me with his intensity. Aunty Pavani had flown back to New York after the first week of felicitations, I was very much alone and vulnerable.

There were two positive results that transpired from my success. The first was that I had to serve out my obligations as the reigning Miss World and abide by the franchise regulations, which did not include a partner. As an ambassador for the franchise under their slogan "beauty with a purpose," I was scheduled to visit many new places and countries, commitments that Lohan had no control over. The second benefit was more personal and arrived in the form of an efficient young lady allocated by the franchise, my own public relations manager. Nisha was British by birth but of Indian origin, and was not only efficient, but diplomatic as well, and was very understanding of my situation. She was adept at keeping Lohan at bay and gradually managed to create a distance between Lohan's presence and my appearances at various events, while I was carrying out my obligations.

It was just a couple of months into my reign while visiting Mumbai, that there was a message at the reception of the hotel I was staying in, requesting for an appointment to meet me on a personal matter. I had many such requests, all of which were vetted by Nisha, but when it was mentioned by her that it was from a young gentleman from Mandvi, it piqued my interest and I was intrigued enough to grant him some time. I was totally unprepared for what followed. He was a charming young man around my age who seemed somewhat embarrassed at the message he had been asked to convey. He said he was an emissary of his grandfather who, on hearing that I wished to visit Mandvi, had issued an invitation as he had something of interest to discuss. The young man seemed quite uncomfortable in his role of the emissary as he presented me with an envelope. Inside it was a photograph, it was an old one, a grainy print in black and white, and as I looked at it I was astounded. I saw my mirror image in a bygone era and felt an affinity to this unknown woman. I sensed a mystery and felt the need to know more of this woman I resembled. I accepted the invitation and asked him to convey to his grandfather that I would contact him as soon as I had the opportunity to travel to Mandvi. The young man left, leaving the photograph and the address and contact number of his grandfather in Mandvi.

The second encounter happened a few weeks later while I was still in Mumbai, and it was far more dramatic. I had just returned to the hotel after a photo shoot and was walking across the lobby towards the elevator, when a tall, handsome, bearded young man, in traditional clothes, strode towards me, thrusting out a small package in his hand. The staff accompanying me and security personnel allocated to me sprang into action and wrestled the young man to the ground while grabbing the parcel from his hand. It was while they were attempting to escort the young man away that I heard him say that his grandfather had requested he deliver the package into my hands in person. This reference to his grandfather, a few weeks after the earlier interaction, did not seem to be a coincidence. So, I asked that I speak to the young man. After frisking him thoroughly and opening the package, I was permitted to meet with the young man in private at one corner of the lobby. This young man, unlike the other, seemed angry and resentful rather than embarrassed at his role as the emissary. He had flown in from Karachi, he did not know the reason, he was just abiding by his grandfather's orders. He was ill at ease and uncomfortable in my presence, a reluctant messenger. He said he had been asked to hand over the package to me in person. Within the parcel were a small box and a letter. I opened the letter first. It contained a few pages written in Urdu, a language I understood but was unable to read. I kept it aside and looked into the little box. Inside lay a bracelet, it was identical to the one I owned. My bracelet was one that had been included in the package of jewellery handed over to me by Aunty Pavani, jewellery that I thought had belonged to my mother. This bracelet was as unique and as spectacular as mine was. I had had mine appraised and I knew it was custom made and extremely valuable. This one in my hand was not a copy, it was its twin. I thanked the young man and attempted to return the bracelet but he was insistent that I made that decision after I had read the letter. He gave me his telephone number and the address at which to contact him in Mumbai and abruptly took my leave, leaving me with the bracelet and in suspense.

Although I could have had the letter translated by one of the staff, I was reluctant to do so as I did not know what it revealed. I felt that something about this mystery somehow involved me, and it needed to stay private. Having some time on my hands the next morning, and after a few discreet inquiries at the reception, I learnt that there was an elders' home nearby where I may find some residents who could decipher the language. I made my way unobtrusively to the address given. An elderly lady there read out the contents to me. Written in an old-fashioned, flowery, and poetic style, it told the story of tragic love. A love story between two people from different worlds, a story of a poor drummer and a dancer, of love that was doomed to fail. There were no names mentioned, but tying it all together was the description of her beautiful eyes and the distinctive bracelet that had belonged to her. I returned to my hotel, with the letter and its tragic love story, holding the valuable bracelet and none the closer to unravelling the mystery. I was now even more determined to solve this intriguing puzzle and its connection to me. I tried to contact the young man, but could not connect to the number he had given. I sent Nisha over to the address he had written to ask him to meet me, but she was informed that the young man was no longer there, he had returned to Karachi the previous night.

I liked being in Mumbai as it was familiar territory and gave me more freedom. Here I felt less restricted, and out of Lohan's suffocating control. Since Ummi's death and my immediate relocation to the United States, I had not spent much time in this city, let alone at my own house. So I arranged some time off and went home. An older Neelam was delighted at my unexpected visit. Coming home made me very emotional, and evoked good memories. It was here I had grown up, had a loving and sheltered childhood, adored by my grandmother who had always been there, keeping me safe. I sat in her room and reflected over how much I owed her for the secure and protected life I had led.

I cannot remember exactly at what age I was aware, or if it was Ummi who had told me, but I had always known I was an orphan. Maybe it was because of the love and security I received from my grandmother while growing up, I had never felt the need to delve into the details of how I was left an orphan. I had always been aware that Ummi had never been married, and that my mother was the adopted child of her friend Mrs Emmerson. Ummi had told me that my mother had died in an accident when I was a toddler. Now, reflecting on this memory, I wonder if I was led to believe or did I assume, that my father had died in that crash too. I had never questioned Ummi about my parents or the past, I had trusted her implicitly. Ummi had often spoken fondly about this place called Mandvi. She had related stories of her childhood and the beauty of this seaside town, always stating her intention of taking me there someday. I had met her childhood friend Aunty Jameela when she had flown in from Colombo to visit Ummi while she was ailing. I was with them when they reminisced about their delightful days growing up in Mandvi. I knew of Ummi's long association with Aunty Pavani, but I could not recall any mention in the past of a girl with the tragic love story or a girl with the strange eyes, the girl I resembled.

Till as such time I left to the United States, I had not been particularly interested in my lineage. But the recent events of the past weeks had awakened in me a desire to know about my parents and a curiosity to uncover any link they had to Mandvi. That afternoon, I rifled through Ummi's cupboards and desks and uncovered nothing that I had not viewed before, yet this afternoon I looked at them with new eyes. A copy of my birth certificate, covered in a waterproof paper and carefully filed away with all my old school reports and prize certificates. I perused the birth certificate and it had as its details: Father- Rowan Andrew MacLachlan, born in Scotland; Mother: Magni Emmerson, born in Mumbai; and it showed no obvious links to Mandvi. The old albums belonging to Mrs Emmerson detailed the childhood of my mother from a cherubic baby to a tall, gawky but attractive teenager, and later into this most beautiful young girl. There were many a newspaper cutting and magazines featuring my mother, all carefully preserved and hoarded by, I presumed, Mrs Emmerson, her mother. Ummi had a few photographs of me, mostly at school events and performances. There were none of me with either of my parents. It was then that it struck me that there were no photographs to mark my parent's wedding although my father appeared in a handful of them taken together with my mother. He was a tall, broad, and solid foreign man, dressed in formal attire, and they looked both happy and relaxed together. I scrutinized these photographs carefully as I wanted to determine a resemblance, and although I assumed, I must have inherited the colour of my eyes and my height from my father, I felt I looked nothing like my striking mother.

Nothing as close to the similarity that had struck me in that first glance, at that grainy black and white image of the mysterious young girl from Mandvi. It was now I realized how little I knew of my parents.

I left Mumbai a few days later without finding out anything more. It was soon after that I embarked on the first of my assignments overseas and the matter was laid to rest till I could find the time to delve into the mystery again.

Nearly a month had gone by after I returned to New Delhi after visiting Cambodia and Myanmar when the past caught up with me once again. It was strange that for someone who had not featured in my thoughts much, and whom until recently I had only fleetingly been curious about, I recognized him as soon as I saw him. I was having breakfast alone at a restaurant in the hotel where I was residing when I became aware of a gentleman observing me from across the room. I glanced up at him and I knew, there was no doubt in my mind, it was the older version of the very gentleman I had seen in those photographs, my father.

I was taken aback, but before I could recover from my initial confusion, he strode across, approached my table and asked my permission to speak. It happened so fast, I was too shocked to refuse and so, he drew up a chair and sat at my table. Mr Rowan Andrew MacLachlan, as he formally introduced himself, was as nervous and ill at ease as me but he came straight to the point. He wanted to know the name of my mother and the date of my birth. In other circumstances, I would have been wary and reluctant to disclose any such information, but on this day I did not hesitate; the question seemed to be of utmost importance. When I answered, he turned pale. He then took my hand in his and stated quietly, almost sadly, that he was my father. He had flown in from Scotland to personally meet me as he had to be certain, he and I were in no doubt it was so.

Since the initial introduction, we met often. I explained him away as an uncle visiting from overseas. He spoke at length about my mother and their relationship. He did not spare himself blame and I believed him when he swore, that he had not believed her when she had written to him about her pregnant state. He described my mother, bringing her to life for me. A vibrant fiery soul, beautiful and spoilt. He said my mother was wilful and used to getting her own way. He said she had always almost religiously taken her birth control medication as she did not want to disrupt her career. He had thought she was resorting to emotional blackmail to get him back when he had received that desperate letter, to which he had not responded. He had loved her dearly but not above his duty.

He had never known her parents, she had never mentioned them. The only mother she spoke of was Mrs Emmerson. He had met my Ummi but had never heard of this place called Mandvi. My mother, as far as he could recollect, had never been there. Other than bringing my mother to life and describing their life at the time they were together, my father could not shed any light on the puzzle I was trying to piece together.

My father was married now and I learnt that I had two younger siblings. He wished to inform them about my existence when he returned, and he made it very clear that he needed to acknowledge me as his daughter and wanted me in his life. I, who had nobody as family, was utterly bewildered. I had grown to like this big, gruff man but there lingered an underlying sense of resentment in my feelings towards him. I had been deprived not only of a father's presence but of a mother's care, and I was not quite ready to accept him, I needed time. When he left, a part of me was sad to see him go, but I was still unsure if I wanted him in my life. I promised that I would consider his request and contact him if ever I was ready to recognize him as my father.

# CHAPTER 15

# SURYA CHANDNI TAARE "MOONLIGHT AND ROSES."

It was well over six months into my reign as the title-holder, and after many sojourns overseas, and at a time when Nisha was planning on returning to the United Kingdom for a fortnight, I pleaded exhaustion myself and requested some time off. Lohan had resumed his pursuit of me with a vengeance and I found it difficult to deter his attention whenever I happened to be in New Delhi. I knew that with Nisha gone, I would not have her presence to act as a shield and was afraid Lohan's behaviour would prove to be impossible to handle. I felt physically and emotionally drained. I confided in Nisha about the situation before she herself departed. She knew of my desire to visit Mandvi, and it was she who suggested I take this opportunity to go there, to get away anonymously, with no publicity, and get some rest.

Ummi's childhood friend Aunty Jameela had mentioned on her last visit that their residence Sagar Manzil had been purchased and converted into a resort, and that is where I planned to stay. Nisha arranged it all, she booked me in under a company name, paid for the stay in advance, and so I managed to slip away and arrive in Mandvi with nobody but Nisha aware of where I was. I flew into Ahmedabad, hired a car, and arrived late one night in Mandvi. The resort was quiet and peaceful. I revelled in my solitary state and the silence around. It was bliss. The first couple of days I kept to my room, catching up on my sleep, lazing in bed listening to music, reading, until I was certain no one had traced my journey here. On the third day, I ventured outside to view this picturesque place. The resort contained individual chalets set apart by hedges full of pink blossoms. The main dining area overlooked the sea. I could smell the ocean.

The next day I felt secure enough to hire a car to explore the town. Covering my hair and wearing a pair of large sunglasses, I ventured out to find places that I remembered had been mentioned by my Ummi in her conversations reminiscing about her past. I drove across the bridge that had stood the test of time, past walls of the old fort, traced landmarks I recalled she had mentioned, an old water tank, a lighthouse, it all seemed so familiar; Ummi's voice rang through my head making Mandvi come alive. I walked through the narrow lanes of the bazaar, the busy vendors tempting me with their wares. Nobody took any note of me, I was anonymous and totally relaxed. The next day I ventured further afield and drove to the Bohri shrine. It was an imposing and well-maintained structure, from here I tried to trace the house Ummi had spoken of with great affection, but I could not locate it. It seemed the neighbourhood had changed over time. I returned to the resort tired but strangely uplifted. I loved this little town. I felt quite at home here. A few days later I ventured further. I remembered Ummi talking of her visit to this summer palace of the Maharaja of a bygone age. It was, she said, the furthest she had been before leaving Mandvi. I had lunch at a beachside restaurant, I stopped to watch a wooden structure of a ship being built on the river. These sights made me feel close to Ummi, and everything I viewed, seemed to have a strange sense of familiarity.

It was after a week had gone by and I was feeling totally comfortable in my new surroundings that I decided to call the number I had been given by the young man from Mandvi. A call I had wanted to make from the first day I had arrived but was apprehensive about. That very same afternoon, a car was sent to collect me from the resort. We drove back over the old wooden bridge, to the entrance of the narrow lanes leading into the bazaar and there, behind high walls and an imposing gate, we pulled up at the entrance of a large house. The house was partially shuttered, dark and gloomy, and unlike every other place in beautiful Mandvi, I did not feel at ease here. A shiver ran down my spine, yet the old gentleman waiting to receive me could not have been more welcoming. He was overcome with emotion when I alighted from the vehicle.

That afternoon, over many cups of tea and spicy dabeli, he related the tragic story of the life and disappearance of his younger sister, the girl with the unusual eyes, the talented dancer, the girl I so closely resembled. The prophecy of an astrologer, her life in isolation, her sudden disappearance, and the sudden death of his mother all poured out from the old man. He was very interested in the unusual bracelet I had worn at the pageant, and although I told him it had belonged to my mother, he had never heard of Mrs Emmerson or my Ummi who had been the only one with any connection to this place. I showed him a photograph of my parents, spoke of my mother who I knew had never been to Mandvi, and he wondered at how she came into possession of that piece of jewellery. His only surmise was that his sister had lost this bracelet at a wedding she had attended, and the bracelet had found its way to Mumbai. He told me that their mother had never recovered after his sister mysteriously vanished from their home and the most probable theory that was believed of his sister's disappearance was of suicide. His beautiful sister had been ill, and suffering from depression, and it seemed likely that she had taken her own life by walking into the sea, an assumption made on account of her footwear being found on the beach. Her body had never been recovered.

His story checked out with the tragic tale recounted in the letter from Karachi, as I knew she had not left Mandvi with the musician. I was uncertain about disclosing the contents of the letter or the existence of the second bracelet that was delivered to me, and I decided I would wait until I knew more about the mystery before enlightening him about these. It now felt like pieces of a jigsaw puzzle falling into place, but there still remained these unexplained links that needed to be connected together before I could solve this puzzle. I visited the old gentleman on a couple of more occasions. He was lonely and loved talking of the days gone by, but mostly he loved sitting by my side and looking at me. I felt Mandvi was the key, my unexplained resemblance, the unusual bracelets were all connected here and maybe, someday in the future, I would learn the truth and then I could give the old gentleman the answers and some solace.

It was the night before I left Mandvi, a place I had grown to love and a place where I strangely felt at home and at peace. I had a solitary dinner at the restaurant overlooking the ocean, there were just two other diners who seemed to be floating business travellers. After my meal, I let myself out and sat at the terrace, listening to the soothing sound of the waves. It was a beautiful moonlit night. It was just past ten at night, the staff were clearing up the restaurant and had turned off most of the lights. I had ordered a cup of coffee, I sat there in the darkness reflecting on everything that had happened in these last six months, I was sad to be leaving.

I smelt him, before I saw him, a smoky, woody masculine fragrance. He was walking up the steps, leading to the terrace from the beach below. A tall shadow with a burning flicker at his fingertips. I had never been one to initiate any conversation but the words just slipped out, a mundane statement, "Smoking kills you know," I said.

"I should know," he replied, "I am studying medicine, and am trying hard to quit."

He had a deeply attractive voice, slightly accented. He pulled out a chair at my table asking if he could join me, he beckoned to a waiter and ordered two more coffees. It was the last order of the night, we were informed when it was brought, and the rest of the restaurant lights were switched out. We sat in the darkness, under the bright moonlight, a few distant flares lit up the beach, low garden lights indicated the way back to the rooms. Two strangers, just silhouettes, strangely at ease, comfortable companions.

We spoke of Mandvi, its history and beauty, he had arrived just the day before and was looking forward to exploring the town. Aakash, as he introduced himself, was from Australia. He too, I learnt, had family ties to this place and was passing through on his way to Africa. He had just completed four years of medical studies and had volunteered to work in Africa for six months before he returned to complete his studies. He asked me about what had drawn me to Mandvi and I had no reservations in talking to him about my Ummi. I told him about her reminisces and my desire to see the places she had spoken so fondly about. The conversation flowed, he was interested and a good listener.

We chatted and laughed and enjoyed each other's company, we did not feel the time flying by. We spoke of life, in general, I confided my uncertainty about my future plans, he was very clear about his. He knew exactly what he wanted in life, he had a sense of purpose in what he hoped to achieve. He understood as I tried to explain the qualms I had, at this crossroads in my life, and he gave me sound advice. Although total strangers, it seemed so natural, this discussion we had about life and hope, in anonymity and under a moonlit sky, we were in complete harmony.

It was long past midnight when we parted our ways. He was leaving the next morning to visit relatives in Bhuj, I was returning to Mumbai to resume my busy schedule. We walked down together, past the swimming pool, towards the chalets, the low garden lights illuminating just our feet. At a junction, we bid each other goodbye and went our separate ways. I left Mandvi very early the next morning. The rest and reflection had done me good. I was clear-headed. Aakash had given me a guideline. I knew now what I needed to do.

# CHAPTER 16

# MEHUL
# "DARK CLOUDS."

Her visit evoked old memories, regrets, and guilt. I was fourteen years old when she was born. I remember being summoned by the matron of our boarding school to be informed of her arrival, I remember being happy when I was told we had a sister. My brothers Rahul and Anil, at twelve and nine years, were not particularly interested in the news.

I had just turned fifteen when we returned to Mandvi for vacations, and her existence strongly registered again with the unpleasant recollection of seeing my father soundly beating an old woman. My little sister was barely a year when my father had decided to send her away, to be brought up by some distant relatives. My mother distraught, assisted by her loyal maid Hajara, had attempted to return to her home town Pune taking the baby with her. The plan had been discovered, the flight thwarted, and the result, a sound beating for Hajara and my mother banished to the back rooms of our residence with my sister. This was when I was first made aware of the prophecy made by the famed astrologer and the reason behind why the three of us brothers were forbidden from having any interaction with our sister.

All my life, from the time I was very young, I had known that my father was a person of immense wealth and importance. As I grew older, I became aware of just how much power and influence he yielded. I also learnt that he was greatly feared and, from an early age, I made sure never to cross him. His word was the law in all matters and violence resulted if one disagreed. My mother, although considered a great beauty, lived in the shadow of my powerful father, all decisions regarding the family were made by him, and she had little influence over him. Yet, with regards to my sister, she had rebelled, and being allowed to keep the baby with her, although at a distance from us, was her one great victory in this union. My brothers and I were sent off to a prestigious boarding school near the capital city of Delhi, at a very young age. My father was very superstitious and greatly influenced by the stars as read by astrologers. As such, when the birth of my sister foretold of malefic influences on the males of the family, he made sure that he and us boys had no contact with her whenever we returned to Mandvi. All I can recall of her as a child was an occasional sighting of a thin and pale toddler playing by herself, in the backyard of the house. I remember feeling sorry for the little girl, but I did not attempt to get close as we had been forbidden from doing so. Being much older, we hardly had any opportunity, as a few years after her birth I was sent off to England to pursue my studies and my brothers followed not long after. My father ensured there was a great distance between us and our only sister.

He himself lived in Ahmedabad, away from any malefic influence she could cast on him.

As boys, our father had already mapped out our future, and for me as the oldest, he had great political ambition. I was around twenty-two years of age when I returned to India with a degree in Engineering. I was immediately absorbed into my father's business and thrust into the political arena as my father desired. I went along as he wished, but it was soon revealed that I was not cut out to shine in both these fields. I was neither driven nor ambitious in business or politics. I enjoyed reading, philosophy, listening to western classical music, and was far more passionate about wildlife and photography. To my father, all my interests were just a waste of time. In a couple of years, my father arranged a suitable partner for marriage, the daughter of a political ally, consolidating a long-standing political alliance. At the age of twenty-five, I married a young girl from the neighbouring city of Bhuj. It was at the wedding ceremonies that I can recall the next memory I have of my sister. A thin, gawky, awkward young girl following closely behind my mother. My marriage proved to be fortunate as I moved to Bhuj and away from my father's oppressive presence. My wife was a kind, simple girl, her parents more understanding and my life too became pleasant and happy. A year later we were blessed with a baby boy.

The next year brought on a calamity upon the family, my brother Rahul informed my father that he had married an English girl, that too in a church. My father was furious, he severed all ties with my brother and forbade us from having any contact with him. I am quite sure he never once considered my mother's feelings about his decision. My youngest brother Anil proved to be a further disappointment. He returned to India before completing his studies. Anil had always been one who enjoyed a life of ease, he settled down in Bombay, where he led a life that was filled with parties, girls, liquor, and later drugs. Surprisingly, my father seemed to turn a blind eye on his lifestyle and probably funded it. On rare occasions when he did visit Mandvi, he was most often drunk and disorderly.

The eldest he considered a loser, the second a lost cause, and the youngest a libertine, my father would have been very disappointed at the three sons he had birthed. He would have considered it a result of the prophecy of gloom, doom, and malefic influence foretold. My brother Anil, after living a life of dissipation, succumbed to cirrhosis of the liver and passed away at the age of fifty. The one joy that my father received from his sons was my son, his only grandson who, from his earliest years, showed all the traits of turning out as a replica of his paternal grandfather. My father doted on him.

After my marriage, I saw my young sister on rare and fleeting visits to Mandvi at festivals. She was as always a shadow hovering in the background. One of my greatest regrets in life was not having the courage to look past the superstition and getting to know her. It was a few years later when my wife and I went to Mandvi to join the family to attend some wedding ceremonies there, that I saw my sister in a totally different light. My sister had transformed from the spindly ugly duckling into a glorious swan. That afternoon, she floated gracefully down the steps behind my stately mother, her long lustrous black hair flowing down to her waist. She looked stunning in her rose-pink attire, a long neck holding up a head held high, her unusual eyes darkened with kohl looked startling. I was blown away by this vision of beauty I beheld. It was the first time I had witnessed my father at a loss of words. He seemed startled, and it was also the first time I saw him acknowledge her. I heard him address her directly about the unusual bracelets she wore, telling her they had been personally designed by his mother and handcrafted by a famous jeweller in Delhi. He asked me to fetch my camera, which I always carried around with me, and requested I take some photographs of my sister.

A couple of days later, I myself accompanied my wife, parents, and sister to the nikah ceremony of the wedding, and I witnessed guests turning to stare at us as we walked past. My wife was pretty and my mother stately, but it was my sister that attracted all that attention. She looked dazzlingly beautiful that night. I remember the day following the wedding well as the next morning my mother asked me to return to the venue. My sister seemed to have mislaid one of those heirloom bracelets, and although Mrs Rajkotwala instructed an army of domestics to scour the house and gardens, there was no trace of the missing bracelet. I left Mandvi with my wife late that evening, I did not see my sister that day and could not bid farewell to her as I was told she was in bed unwell. That dazzling vision was my last sight of her and that is how she would always be etched in my memory, and how I would remember her, for just about two months after that day, my sister disappeared.

It was early one morning that I was awakened by my wife with news of urgent summons to Mandvi by my distraught mother. It was there, amongst the confusion, disarray, and mayhem, that I was informed that my sister could not be found. My father arrived from Ahmedabad and although the city was combed from end to end, the domestics and the gatekeepers beaten and questioned, nothing yielded results. My sister seemed to have vanished without a trace. Rumours of kidnapping, elopement, and murder abounded but nobody unravelled the mystery of her disappearance. There had been no talk, no opportunity to develop a secret liaison, no ransom notes or demands for her return were issued, no body surfaced, but a day later, a pair of slippers were found on the beach, and were attributed by Hajara the maid as belonging to my sister, which pointed to the theory of suicide. Not a person had seen her leave or walk towards the beach, but her long illness, her depressed mental condition, the footwear found on the beach, all led to the assumption that my sister had wilfully taken her own life.

My mother fell ill after my sister disappeared. She took to her bedroom and never left it. She fell into a deep depression. A week after the futile search, my father returned to Ahmedabad and I back to Bhuj, leaving behind a house of misery, with the mysterious disappearance never fully explained, or death never fully determined. Suffering from deep guilt for not caring enough to visit my sister while she was unwell, I drove to Mandvi often to visit my mother, but she did not speak a word after that fateful day and never ever recovered from the loss of my sister.

A little over six months after my sister disappeared, my mother passed away. My wife and I were away overseas at the time. The reasons for her demise were never disclosed as my father had her body cremated very soon after. Although most people said that overcome with grief, my mother had pined away, I heard from a domestic who worked in the house at the time that she had taken her own life and my father had the matter hushed up. With the tragedy of the two deaths, another mystery unfolded as the disappearance of all my mother's jewellery came to light. This resulted in another round of beatings and questioning but the inquiries yielded nothing. The family home was shuttered and shut. My father had attempted to send Hajara back to Pune, but she had refused to move. She lived out her years at the back rooms of the house, a sad old woman who spent her days tending my mother's grave. Everyone considered her insane as she kept rambling about a lost baby in Bombay.

Today, when I have the time to reflect on the past, my thoughts are often filled with thoughts of my dear mother and sister, and the tragic unexplained events that unfolded so many years ago. My brother Rahul estranged, Anil deceased, and myself a recluse, the malefic prediction of doom and gloom could be seen as proven to be true. But although his sons had proved to be a disappointment, as the years rolled by, my father lived to see his dream fulfilled through his grandson. My only son proved to be a chip off the old block, inheriting not only his business acumen and drive but also his ambition and ruthlessness. My father lived to see my son enter the parliament before he died. He is now a minister in the State of Gujarat.

When I lost my dear wife, I decided to return to the ancestral house in Mandvi which I had inherited. Here I live peacefully, a life of routine, a life filled with some happy memories and plagued with some regrets, surrounded by my books, music, and countless albums of my photographs.

# CHAPTER 17

# ZAAHEB
# "ALL THAT GLITTERS."

Igrew up on the streets of Karachi, an abandoned child, running around with a band of other children like myself, but I stood out amongst them as I was extremely fair and possessed fiery red-gold hair. We lived in squalor and scavenged for food, and it was a common practice, among us children, to sneak into the kitchens of the many wedding halls in the city to forage for scraps to eat. It was at one such wedding that I heard a band of musicians performing and I was mesmerized by the sound. Music struck a chord within me and ever since that day, I liked to hang around this troupe wherever they performed around the city. The musicians soon got accustomed to me following them around and the leader of the troupe, an older man, was particularly kind towards me. One cold and rainy night, I think he felt sorry for my plight and took me to his house into shelter. He lived with his wife, his own children all long gone about with their own lives. From that fortunate night, I lived with this couple, a roof over my head and off the streets. They fed me, clothed me, and cared for me like their own and, for this, I owed them all the gratitude and loyalty I could give.

I must have been around seven or eight years old at the time and Barbar, my saviour, was in his sixties. Barbar gave me my name Zaaheb which he told me meant golden in the Farsi language, for up to that time I had always been called bachcha, a child with no parents and no name, a nobody.

I accompanied Barbar and the musicians everywhere, fetching and carrying, and doing various errands and odd jobs and they, in return, recognized my interest in music and taught me to master some of the musical instruments. I liked them all, but I enjoyed and later excelled in all forms of percussion. For the next ten years, my life was centred around music, musicians in Barbar's troupe may have changed over time but Barbar still led the troupe, with me now being a permanent fixture in it. The troupe had over time also gained recognition and was much in demand to perform at various celebrations. When I was around fifteen or sixteen years old, at one of these gatherings I was introduced to a group of young men who befriended me. They were somewhat hot-headed and held strong political opinions. I was excited by their views, some of which seemed quite radical. I liked their company and joined their group voluntarily, not particularly because I believed in their cause but because they gave me a feeling of brotherhood and belonging. Barbar disapproved but he did not attempt to forbid me from keeping their company, I think he realized I was at the age of rebellion, asserting my independence, and I am sure he felt my interest would wane over time. I continued my performances with the troupe and my initial contribution to my new found brotherhood was purely gathering random information from the various venues we played at. Sometime later, I graduated to becoming a courier, never knowing what it was that I carried across the city.

It was while we were performing at an exclusive and elaborate Mehendi ceremony in Karachi that a wealthy lady from across the border heard us play. She had particularly enjoyed our repertoire of ghazals and invited Barbar to perform at her daughter's nuptials in the neighbouring town of Mandvi in India. I think more than the very generous remuneration offered along with accommodation, it was the excitement of the musicians to travel across the sea that persuaded Barbar to accept the offer. I, too, was thrilled at the idea of travelling across by boat, as I had never been outside of my city. I must have been around nineteen at the time, and with my physique and long golden hair was considered very handsome by my mates and fellow musicians. I had many young and older ladies from all walks of life, who attempted to entice me into a relationship, but I was a romantic at heart and their lures did not appeal or tempt me. My mates and the older musicians were amused and often laughed at my expense calling me "a fool."

We arrived in Mandvi six months later and two weeks prior to the wedding ceremonies. We were provided accommodation at a school that was closed at the time for the vacation. The little town was fascinating to a city boy like me and I had fun exploring around with my friend and fellow musician Salim. We were both young and adventurous, excited to be in India and to be performing at a large gathering of dignitaries. It was a couple of days after we arrived that, one afternoon, we were asked to provide music for a dance lesson that was held on the school premises. It was an opportunity for the troupe to practice as well; we were all tuning up the musical instruments when a group of giggly young girls were ushered in by their dance teacher.

She came in last, she walked with such grace, a swan among a gaggle of geese. I had never seen a girl as beautiful as her before. I could not take my eyes off her. It was as if I had been punched hard in the stomach, I was winded and could not breathe. I wanted to touch her to make sure she was not just a figment of my imagination and, eventually, I could not help myself; I stopped drumming and walked up behind her, I could not help touching her, and maybe it was the shock of it due to which she collapsed into my arms. My heart was pounding as I lay her down gently and walked away. I had never felt such a powerful emotion, it was exhilarating. My fellow musicians teased me endlessly that evening. They suspected that I was smitten by that beautiful dancer, but they also let me know of the consequences. She was the only daughter of the most powerful and feared man in all of Gujrat. They warned me that I would be in danger of a sound beating if ever he got word that I had touched her. Every warning went unheeded, it was as if an addictive drug had entered my bloodstream. I could not get her off my mind. I had to see her, speak to her, nothing could deter my intention of making contact.

It was easy to find out the schedule for the next lesson of dance classes. I scouted around the school for a place where I could meet her without arousing suspicion. On the morning of the next dance class, I pleaded a headache and excused myself from the troupe's practice session. Instead, I sat at the back of the class, near the door from which she exited, and gazed at her throughout the lesson. I knew she would leave to collect her belongings outside the door as soon as the class was done. I slipped out quietly behind her and slipped the note I had written into her hand. Our eyes met, we did not speak a word but the intensity of the feeling between us was electrifying. She clutched the note tightly and she did not thrust it back at me, she did not object, I was elated.

I had decided on the last of the classrooms down a long corridor for the tryst. It had a secluded alcove at the back, hidden from view at the entrance. I did not know if she would come, I had no plan on what I was going to say if she did, I had no bad intentions in my mind. I waited by the entrance, my nerves stretched on tenterhooks and then she was there. I did not say a word, I took her by the hand and led her to the alcove, as I turned around to look at this beautiful sight, she melted into my arms. Words were not needed, she lifted her face and my lips met hers. There was this exciting chemistry between us, it was like a bolt of electricity passing through and exploding into fiery passion. I was aroused mentally and physically, her body pressed tightly against me. I had never experienced anything as exciting before, it was electrifying. In all her innocence, she did not realize the physical effect she had on me. I could not control my reaction, it was satisfying. I hurriedly sat on a low desk and sat her down on my lap. I stroked her hair and spoke to her of her beauty, of my love. I recited verses of poetry to convey my feelings and made her promise to meet me there again.

By the time of the following dance class, I had managed to smuggle in a large quilt and a few cushions into the alcove. This time when I led her there, I gently lay her down. When I kissed her, the passion ignited once again, I could not control myself, I wanted to possess her, to make her mine, and I rolled on top of her. She did not resist, she seemed as eager as I was to be one. When it was done, I held her close and told her how much I loved her, I told her I needed to take her away with me and promised we would be together forever. I vowed to make all the arrangements and I had every intention of doing so.

I scouted around the next few days, speaking to the locals at the bazaar about finding a passage to Karachi and finally met one who directed me to a particular area from where they ferried people across the sea illegally. The boatman I spoke to was very clear, it could be done for a dear amount. I fixed the date and time and booked passage for two, and was now only needed to raise the required finances. I had made friends with one of the drivers at Sagar Manzil where we now had regular practices and he had agreed to take me to the rendezvous spot on that night for a small fee. I did not mention a second passenger but I knew I could persuade him at the time. I tried at first to raise the money from my fellow musicians but they did not possess excess money and I could not give them any reason for requiring the funds. Although the excitement of meeting my beloved and the amazement at her astonishing beauty on the night of the Mehendi ceremony moved me, the weight of my monetary situation bore me down as I led her to a spot I had discovered on my earlier visits to the venue. It was well-hidden by the overhanging branches of the shrubs growing wild. Here I possessed her once more, my overwhelming desire overcoming all the discomfort. She trusted me completely and I knew I could not let her down. I spoke to her of my plans, the arrangements I had made, and I swore I would raise that money even if I had to steal it. I promised her once again that we would be together forever. I did not ask, although the thought did cross my mind, and it must have struck her too as she saw me gaze at it. She slipped a bracelet off her wrist and placed it in my hand, she did not hesitate for one moment, she wanted to be with me forever too. I was very excited when I left the ceremony that night, everything seemed to be falling into place. The only mistake I made was taking my friend Salim into my confidence. Salim was more worldly than me, he knew the art of bargaining and getting a fair deal, and I knew nothing of the value or how to get about pawning jewellery. So that night I told him of my intention and my plan. The bracelet itself, I did not show him as it was safely tied to the cord of my loose pants under my long Kurta. In the early hours of the next morning, I was held down, a cloth stuffed into my mouth, and my hands and feet bound by rope. As much as I struggled, there were too many of them, I was trussed up and left in a room I could not move from or make a sound in. A couple of hours later they returned. The sun was up and I could see all the members of the troupe and with them Barbar. He removed the cloth from my mouth, I railed, I begged, I cried but to no avail. He waited till I was spent and then he spoke.

He told me that Salim had gone to him with my story and he had done so because he was my friend and was worried about me. He explained why he could not let me carry out my plan. He said even if I managed to leave with her undetected on the night of the Nikah ceremony, her disappearance would be apparent in just a couple of hours when the guests were ready to depart. The missing drummer would soon be noticed. He told me that I would be putting everyone in the troupe at the risk of imprisonment, even death. He needed to remind me of the fearful reputation of her father and the repercussions and retribution that would follow. Barbar said he was responsible for all the musicians, most of whom were family men with wives and children. He could not let me go ahead with my scheme and put every one of them in danger. I wailed and sobbed, but deep within me I knew everything he said was true, I understood the disaster I would be bringing upon them all. They untied me but left me locked up in the room. I did not attempt to get out, there was nowhere I could go. I lay on my mat, I did not eat or speak, my dreams were shattered. The next afternoon, just prior to leaving for Sagar Manzil for the wedding ceremony, Barbar came in to see me with a flask and two mugs. He spoke to me, he promised me that he would seek her out and explain. He poured out the tea into the mugs and handed me one. I was thirsty, tired, and broken. Barbar and the tea were comforting, I drank the tea.

I felt the bobbing before I regained consciousness, it felt soothing, this gentle rocking motion, it took me a while to realize I was trussed up once again, the waves gently rocking me across the ocean, away from my beloved, back to Karachi. I left Barbar and the troupe and never performed again. I re-joined the movement but this time I got actively involved, and now I insisted on payments for assignments I carried out. I was determined to collect the money required to return to Mandvi and bring her back with me. It took me over a year of clandestine operations before I amassed what I thought was enough money to return. I had changed over that year, I was tougher, bolder, and shrewder, and I was convinced nothing would stop me now.

When I made that journey back to Mandvi, nothing prepared me for the heartbreak I felt, when I heard of the tragic outcome of my desertion, the students at the dance class enlightened me. I had lost my beloved once again, this time forever.

I returned to Karachi and the movement was all I had. I threw myself wholeheartedly into the cause and rose up in the ranks of the organization, till eventually, I became their esteemed leader.

A few years later, a marriage was arranged for me. She was the sister of a fellow member, an innocent, kind woman who made a good wife but never again did I feel that burning desire or passion I had for my beloved first love. At the birth of my only daughter, I finally came to terms with my loss, I made a decision to move on and paid a visit to Barbar and his wife. Barbar had retired and spent his days quietly at home. I was glad I could provide them with some comfort in the final years of their life. My only daughter married at a young age and birthed a lusty boy with golden hair, he was the pride and joy of my life.

The bracelet was the only link I had with the past and my beloved. I never presented it to my wife or daughter. I had it enclosed in a large locket and it hung from a chain around my neck, resting always close to my heart.

## CHAPTER 18

# ROWAN ANDREW MACLACHLAN "ROOTS."

I was born five years after my brother Arthur, the second son of an illustrious and titled family, from the Northern Highlands of Scotland. We lost our father when we were still very young, I was just five years at the time and my older brother was everything to me; I hero-worshipped him. We were both physically similar in appearance, tall, broad, and red-headed, but this was where the similarity ended, for while he was a born leader, engaging in all the outdoor activities of rugby, archery, and hunting, I loved to read, enjoyed listening to music, and visiting museums. Ours was an old and noble family who had originally been farmers and landowners but my grandfather, a forward-thinking shrewd man, had set up a small distillery using the grains we cultivated. Over two generations, this small operation had grown into one of the most renowned brands of scotch whiskey produced, and us into very wealthy men. My mother was a formidable woman with a forceful personality who ran the estate and the business efficiently till my brother came of age to take control. She adored her firstborn son, whom she considered to be everything a son should be, but she did not understand me, her second born, the one who preferred wine to whiskey and books and music to horses and sports.

As the second-born, I was not of paramount importance to the title and had no particular personal interest in the estate and business. I wanted to study arts and literature, travel and see the world. My brother had been groomed from an early age by my autocratic mother, to shoulder his birth right and his inheritance, and I was very happy to leave all that, in his capable hands. I chose to go to university and left to join one soon after my schooling was done. I was a good student and welcomed the freedom of living an independent and carefree life. After I graduated, I wished to join the foreign services and explore the world. My brother, unlike my mother, understood my nature and my wish to distance myself from her stifling influence and encouraged me to live as I wished. It was he who used his influence to get me a good post in a large multinational company. This was much against my obsessive mother's wishes but my brother intervened and, eventually, I moved away to the city to take up the offer. Initially, I worked in the city office for a few years where I found the work interesting but not exciting, and eventually, I was offered a chance to take up a posting in the firm's branch in India. I jumped at this opportunity and looked forward to travelling to Bombay. My dear brother had by this time settled on a life partner and married a girl born and brought up in the same mould as my mother, and thus ensured that the line of succession was secure. My mother thankfully did not raise much objection to my departure overseas.

It was away from the stifling conventions into the stifling heat but I took to my life in India with great pleasure. Mornings spent in an old colonial office building and evenings with fellow expatriates in old colonial clubs, it was a life of comfort and ease. I enjoyed reading about the rich history of the land, I liked learning about the culture and loved visiting historical and heritage sites, palaces, and temples. When I returned to Scotland after a year, I found life back home cold and dampening, and longed to return. I had got accustomed to a different lifestyle in the East.

It was at a popular bar that I literally bumped into her. She was startlingly beautiful, with her red-gold hair cascading down her bareback, and her emerald green eyes matching the shimmering, figure-hugging short dress. I realized she was tipsy as she openly flirted with me. The couple at whose invitation I was at that bar, was not amused at the behaviour of this brazenly forward young girl and, very soon after, I was obliged to leave the bar with them. In the days that followed, I regretted that decision as I could not get her vision out of my mind. It was a couple of months later, while at the races, that I saw her again. She was walking majestically down the ramp for a renowned designer and this time I did not let the opportunity to introduce myself pass by. I made every effort to charm that beautiful young girl. It started as a casual romantic fling, an unlikely relationship between a solid, staid Scotsman, and a wilful, stunning young model, but as time passed I realized I enjoyed her liveliness, her youthful adoration, she lit up my life and I grounded her. We were soon lovers and a couple, and when signs of permanence became more apparent, is when I had to face up to the prejudices of the time.

Initially, my friends in the expatriate community were polite. They tolerated my interest and her presence, assuming that my infatuation would not last. There was a lot of envy and back-slapping among the gentleman, ribald jokes and suggestions, but when it became clear that she had become a fixture in my life, their attitudes changed and the prejudices surfaced, they closed ranks and made it apparent that she was not welcome in their circle. The other strata of society which showed displeasure at our relationship came from the domestics that were employed at my residence. While they bent in two over any of my Caucasian female associates, I noticed that there was an underlying sense of insolence in their service towards her. Circumstances combined to change the nature of our relationship. There were two particular unrelated incidents that opened my eyes to her situation. One morning I overheard my houseboy refer to her in a derogatory manner which resulted in me having to dispense with his services, and soon after, while we were dining out together we ran into an expatriate couple I had socialized with previously and they pointedly ignored her presence. It was then that I myself had to confront the direction of our future relationship and decided to take steps to remedy the situation. Having her feel disrespected while sleeping over at my residence, or facing the embarrassment of booking into hotel rooms was no longer appropriate. She mattered more to me than my circle of friends and associates. I rented out an apartment in a residential and prestigious neighbourhood and we moved in as a couple together. Here we could relax and be together in each others company, in our own little world. Here we were not judged by society or people who did not matter to us, here in our own space we were blissfully happy.

A year after I met Magni and a couple of months after we moved in together, I returned to Scotland for my annual leave. Word of my alliance with a young model had preceded my arrival and reached the ears of my brother. Once again, I was accosted with much back-slapping and ribald jokes among our friends, nobody considered the relationship serious. My brother and his wife insisted on inviting suitable and eligible young women from 'our set,' as they referred to them, to meet me, but I found their company dull and boring and gently rebuffed any talk of the future. I could not wait to get back, I missed her beautiful presence and vibrant personality. She stood out like a fiery beacon as she waited to greet me at the airport on my return, she flung her arms around me joyfully, she had missed me as much as I had her. We settled back into our comfortable routine. We did not crave going out, we liked being together in our apartment, happy and content in each other's arms.

The next year was one in which we grew closer together. Magni herself had matured, no longer craving attention and high living. She was happy to return home after assignments and lead a quieter and more domesticated lifestyle. We spent weekends away, holidaying and visiting places of interest. I encouraged her to visit her ailing mother and, after some time, she took me along to meet her. She was a lovely lady who adored her daughter and seemed happy that I was in her life. When Magni lost her mother, she turned to me for comfort and support. I provided the security she needed and she depended on me and loved me for it. I knew she loved me and I loved her too, yet I was reluctant to make a commitment and was fearful of making the relationship official. I was hesitant to make that final declaration of love as I knew of the prejudices that we would have to face if I decided to make the union permanent.

Magni wished to accompany me back to Scotland on my next furlough, but I decided it would not be a wise move at the time. I knew her reception in my house would be frosty. I wanted to prepare them, to inform my mother and brother of my intention of marrying Magni, before I introduced her to them. I wanted to shield her, protect her from any slights she might face, I knew my mother and sister-in-law well, Magni would not have easy conquest or acceptance there. Neither my mother, brother, nor my brother's wife took the news of my intention well. My mother forbade the mention of Magni's name in her presence. My brother, who had always indulged me, was surprisingly harsh and firmly opposed any talk of marriage. It was later that he explained to me that his wife had just undergone a third miscarriage and he was a worried man. My mother, my brother, and his wife were under severe stress, all caught up in old beliefs of traditions, bloodlines, and lines of succession. My mother made it very clear that if I went ahead and married Magni, I would be severing ties with everyone I loved and revered, everything that was familiar and precious to me in Scotland.

It was with a heavy heart that I returned to Bombay. I was torn between two worlds. I knew I loved Magni but I was not ready to risk the life I was born into, to marry her. I was unsure if I was ready or able to give it all up for her. This time, on my return, our relationship was somewhat strained. Although I did not mention it, Magni sensed my uncertainty, she recognized the evasion and I understood my lack of courage to face up to the consequences. Then, a few months later, fate took a hand in my life and future, it came in the form of an urgent telephone call from Scotland. I was informed that my dear brother had been thrown off his horse and was seriously injured. I returned to Scotland immediately and learnt it was a head injury and was life-threatening. My once strong and forceful mother was a broken shell of what she had been. She had aged, withered, a helpless old woman I did not recognize, and my dear sister-in-law, a shadow of herself. I had to step in, be strong and, for the first time in my life, shoulder the burden of responsibility. I did not have time to think of myself, let alone Magni, although I did call her to inform her about my brother's condition, and when I was feeling very low, I wished she was there with me to confide my fears and give me comfort. My beloved brother never did regain consciousness, he breathed his last with me at his bedside. Arthur, who had been my rock, my support in life, and although not many years my senior, was like the father I did not remember, was gone. I was devastated and I was now also the head of the family, the laird of the land.

It was the most difficult decision I made, it was also the most difficult letter I penned, yet I had come to terms with the fact that I could no longer be the carefree younger son that set off joyfully to India. I had inherited the title, the lands, the business, and with it all the responsibilities that came with that birth right. I was brutal, I did not want to give her false hope. She was still so young, so beautiful, I hoped she would forgive me, forget me, and move on. I loved her but there was no future in it for us together. I resigned my post, discontinued the telephone line, took no calls, and made a clean and painful break.

Her letter arrived a month or so later. I had still not reconciled to my elevated status in life or recovered from the shock of losing my brother. I read it and saw it only as a desperate appeal, an attempt at emotional blackmail, for I recalled the wilful girl who did not take rejection well and always wanted her own way. I remembered the fact that Magni had been religiously particular about birth control due to her career, I did not believe her claim and did not acknowledge or reply to that letter. I immersed myself in the business, shouldering all the responsibilities, as I needed to forget the loss of the only two people whom I had loved in my life.

My mother never recovered from the death of her firstborn and favourite son, she followed him to her grave a year later. My sister-in-law remained in the castle, running the household as efficiently as expected. After a couple of years passed by, she invited and arranged for a distant cousin to visit. Emma was a sweet, timid girl from a good bloodline. She subsequently made a suitable wife and produced two children, my daughter Fiona and the heir my young son Arthur, thus ensuring succession, the symbol of continuity.

# CHAPTER 19

# LOHAN
# "FIST OF IRON."

I grew up resenting my own mother. My father, I never knew, he was not around; my mother gave me everything I asked for but not her time. It was my grandfather who was always there for me, but he was no substitute for the love, care, and security a mother can give her child. I grew up having anything I wished for, my demands were constant and grew outrageous, but I always got whatever I asked for. It was my way of seeking attention from my mother and it was her way of compensating for her lack of time and attention towards me.

As a precocious rich child, I had plenty of children who hung around me in school but I never had a friend, and by the time my twelfth birthday rolled around, I had become a thoroughly indulged and spoilt boy and it came as a shock when I was suddenly packed off to a boarding school in England. It was a decision made by my mother on my behalf and I hated her for it, as I was thoroughly unhappy there. I who had ruled over an army of servile domestics and staff, I who was used to always having my own way, was suddenly thrust into this world of rules and regulations. A world in which I was considered an 'outsider,' and referred to disparagingly as,

brownie, darkie, or chocolate. The most unkind beings
are children and I learnt it the hard way in the boarding
school. I was bullied from the start for daring to assume
I was better than the others. The older boys considered
me arrogant, insolent, and 'needing to be brought down
a peg,' and they made sure I did. I who up to that point
in my life had been waited on hand and foot, I who
had never done anything on my own was made to serve
others. It was here, at an early impressionable age, that I
developed this obsession about skin colour, it was here I
started to equate fair skin with superiority, a fixation that
I carried throughout my life.

I was miserable for the first two years at the school,
I never mentioned it or complained, and it was only
my grandfather who sensed that something was amiss.
He had retired from his business commitments and
relocated to live in London. I spent my vacations with
him, travelling to visit places of interest in Europe. It was
he who realized my unhappiness, he who delved into the
cause and devised a way out. He asked me to invite the
one boy who gave me the hardest time in school to join
me on my next vacation to Switzerland. I invited the
biggest bully of them all. He came from a broken family
himself, a son of parents who were both doctors, and he
too probably lacked personal attention from his parents
like me. He too came from a wealthy background but
not in the league of my grandfather. We flew first class,
we stayed in the most luxurious resorts, my grandfather
flaunted his wealth, he commanded service and attention

and had Caucasian personnel scurrying to please our every whim. The young bully was impressed, and when I returned my status was established and I had learnt the power of money. I could buy them all. I was fifteen and from that early age, I used money to buy favours, friends, prestige, and influence. I settled in happily at school.

I had occasionally returned to Bombay for short periods during my school days but I did not like being there. I found the city dirty, crowded, and looked down upon it all. I preferred my life in England. It was when I turned fifteen, and on a visit back in India, my mother informed me that I had to stay a short time with my father while I was back. I did not want to see him but she insisted that under court order it was compulsory that I complied. When I did travel to Delhi and met him, I did not like what I saw. He was a sickly, dissipated looking individual, who I was reluctant to acknowledge as my father. He was ailing but I did not feel any sympathy for him, I only was sickened by him. It was for the first time I felt thankful to my mother for keeping me away from my father. I spent two weeks in New Delhi and the only positive outcome of the visit was the preference I developed for that city over my hometown Bombay. Every day that I spent with my father, with his complaints, whining, and demands for money, I grew to appreciate my mother, and thankfully that was the only time I saw him, for six months later he passed away and was out of my life.

I grew up from being an angry, resentful boy into a cold, detached, introverted man. I prized the title arrogant. It was difficult for me to form any relationships and the only person I had any attachment to was my grandfather, the one who had shown me the value of having money, to buy what you want. My grandfather died when I was in my early twenties, leaving me wealth that made me among the most sought after bachelors in India. But this inheritance came with a price, I had to return to live in India. Although I had inherited shares in many companies that were already established and successful, I decided that I needed to be on my own. I had never liked life in Bombay, I wished to distance myself from my mother, so I settled on moving to New Delhi and diversified into the advertising business, setting up my own agency. When I initially returned to Bombay after my grandfather's demise, my mother tried to remedy the distance between us while escorting me to view all the existing factories and retail outlets we owned and operated, but I could not develop a closer relationship with her.

Over the next few years my business flourished, and The Agency hired the most beautiful models and actresses in India to market various high-end products. I squired many of them to launches and galas but was never attracted physically to any of them. They were to me just another commodity to trade in. I preferred dating white-skinned foreign girls, but I was mostly emotionally detached, found them too opinionated and forward, and shed them as fast as I acquired them. Yet, I had this obsession, it was an image I had in my head, an image I visualized, even fantasized about. The perfect model to represent my agency and me. An Indian girl, innocent, conservative, traditional and yet, coloured by my prejudices, someone who looked English. A face that would represent modern India in appearance only but remain conventional by nature. A face that could launch a thousand products for my business, but belong exclusively to me, and then she entered my life, and it was my mother who presented my dream girl to me.

She was tall, slim but shapely, skin like porcelain, lustrous blue-black hair, and blue-green eyes. She walked with the grace of an Indian classical dancer, angelic, ethereal, and demure. She was everything I had imagined and more, unique and amazingly beautiful.

Although I assessed her as a business asset and a representative of my agency, I knew she would be that and much more, as for the first time an unfamiliar emotion stirred in me. It was her innocence, the look of an untouched virgin that appealed to me, but what piqued my attention the most was that she was aloof towards me. I who had always been considered a prized catch, and was used to having the most beautiful girls vying for my attention, was unprepared for her total lack of interest in me. She, like myself, was all business and showed no signs of personal attachment. This reaction, this rejection, roused my interest in her. Here was this young, meek girl I felt I could mould exactly as I wished and eventually, when I felt the time was right, I would make mine. She would belong only to me, she would be the ultimate possession.

Initially, I left her alone, I felt I needed to give her time and space but when at a party a young buck started flirting with her, I was surprised myself, at the anger I felt. I realized that I needed to isolate her, I needed to brand her as mine to keep other men away from her. Up until then, I had kept my relationship professional but with her rising popularity, my feelings were changing. I never imagined that I would react with such violence when, one morning, I was handed a tabloid magazine with a photograph of her in the company of an upcoming film star. I had never felt such emotions towards any woman in my life, I did not recognize it as jealousy. The more she drew away, the more I was determined to control and possess her. I did not recognize her first act of rebellion as one, as it was one that appealed to me. Her act to apply and subsequently be selected to participate in the Miss India Contest appeared to be a good idea. I was in no doubt she would win, and I only thought about the prestige the title would bring. A badge of recognition for owning the best, the envy of other men. I did not realize at the time it would be just the beginning of her growing sense of independence.

It was after she won the title, and was to represent the country in the upcoming world contest when it became apparent to me that I was losing control. I held no sway in the organization of the events around the international competition. I had been politely rebuffed by the organizers of the said event. I was not absolutely confident of her ultimate success there, I did not attend the Miss World pageant. Her eventual victory speech was the first indication that she had distanced herself from me personally. It was to me an open act of defiance. I knew then, I had to rein her in, this time I would not wait, I would make it official, she would be given no choice. As soon as her reign was over, she would be vulnerable once again, her public appearances would be over, she would belong only to me. On her return, I tried to impose my will, to get back control, but as the months passed I had to face the reality that she had changed. She was no longer that shy, insecure, dependent, demure young girl that she was, she had gained confidence and become this strong, independent, articulate woman whom I could no longer bend to my will.

She no longer fit the image of the perfect Mrs Lohan Mehta.

# CHAPTER 20

# AAKASH
# "THE SKY IS THE LIMIT."

I, Aakash Ahamed, could have kicked myself when I awoke the morning after I met her. I rushed over to the reception desk but she had already checked out. The receptionist was not much help. Her room had been booked and paid for by a company. She was not registered under the name she had introduced herself the night before. I only knew her as Taare, and I could not believe I had not got a number to contact her. All I had was the memory of her melodious voice and the fragrance of roses, then I remembered she had mentioned a grandmother from Mandvi and the uncertainty of her future plans, a few sketchy details to work on.

I, who had always considered myself a man about town, who was nicknamed Alpha, who had a reputation as a 'player' back in the country I lived, was at a loss for the first time in my life. I had grown up having every advantage life had to offer, a secure home, a sound education, and good looks. I was the only adored son of parents who had chosen to migrate to my beautiful homeland. My father was a doctor who was originally from Ahmedabad, and my mother a nurse also of Indian origin born in Perth. Theirs had been a love story that had withstood great opposition as they were of different faiths. A marriage that had faced many trials until their families were reconciled with my birth, the beloved son and grandson.

On my arrival in Bhuj to visit my relatives, I mentioned the moonlit encounter over lunch to a table full of uncles, aunts, and cousins. They were thoroughly enthralled and were full of interested queries. Was she fair? dark? Indian? foreign? All I could contribute was the fact that she possessed a grandmother who was called Bhoomi and had been from Mandvi. My elderly grand uncle, who we assumed was dozing in one corner of the room and up until that time, as I had been made to understand, was hard of hearing, suddenly spoke out claiming Bhoomi to be his sister. My grandfather and his brother did not possess a sister, so his rambling on about a playmate was attributed by the others, to the early onset of dementia.

When I left Bhuj and arrived in Ahmedabad, I tried to get the mysterious Taare and my missed opportunity out of my mind, but she was difficult to forget. At the first opportunity I got, I mentioned to my grandfather of my grand uncles reminisce about a playmate named Bhoomi. My grandfather remembered her as a childhood playmate as well, but he had lost touch with her after he had moved away from Mandvi. I wondered if this was a strange coincidence, sometimes truth being stranger than fiction. I wished I could have spoken to her of my discovery, I wished I had a way of contacting her, I wished I could meet her again.

I landed in Africa and my work kept me occupied, pushing all regrets aside, but on some nights under the spectacular moonlit skies of Africa, thoughts of her would surface again and I would wonder where she was. It was about three months later, and halfway into my internship when the level of excitement in our little camp rose to a fever pitch. One of the chief benefactors of this welfare project being the 'Miss World' franchise, we were to expect a visit from the current title-holder. On the day of her expected arrival, I had helped deal with the emergency delivery of a very young girl, barely in her teens. It was a premature birth, the infant stillborn, and I was shattered. The arrival of the beauty queen was far from my mind and I had planned to avoid the ceremony altogether. Yet superiors insisted that we all attend and so, I stood in line with all the other excited medical staff to await the beauty.

I saw the motorcade stop at a distance and a girl step out in jungle green safari attire with a wide-brimmed hat. The young children surged forward singing and dancing as they greeted her. She was hidden from view by an army of photographers while she walked down the line shaking hands with the local dignitaries. Just as she reached me, a young toddler broke through the crowds and ran towards her with a flower in her hand. She crouched down to hug the little girl and when she stood up, she looked into my eyes and said, "I hope you have quit smoking."

I heard her voice and I was sure. I was struck dumb, shell shocked, I could not speak. I just grinned from ear to ear as she passed along. This time I made sure I met her again as soon as the felicitations and speeches were done. This time I made no mistake, this time I got every contact detail possible. Her name I did not have to ask.

# CHAPTER 21

# SURYA CHANDNI TAARE "NEW MOON RISING."

It was at the crack of dawn, I left Mandvi to get back to Mumbai. The rest and relaxation had benefited me physically but the conversation with the unknown Aakash had given me a guideline into my future. I was clear-headed, I knew what I needed to do, and I set off with a definite sense of purpose.

There were two people I had to face up to. I had to let Aunty Pavani know that although I owed her much gratitude, I was not under any obligation to live the life she had chosen for me. When Aunty Pavani returned to Mumbai, I spoke to her frankly and openly, she understood, she knew her son.

I dreaded meeting Lohan, but he was surprisingly undisturbed. I explained that after my reign was done I would not be returning to the agency or a career in modelling. I told him, although I was thankful for the opportunities I had been given, this was not the life I had chosen or wanted. I wanted to stand on my own and make decisions for myself regarding my future. I needed to move on. I think Lohan too had realized that I was not the same demure, beholden girl he knew; this new confident, assertive person was not what he envisaged in his life. I was no longer that ideal dream girl he sought and so, we parted ways surprisingly quite amicably.

For someone who I had met just once, it was funny how often Aakash kept intruding my thoughts. I wished I could tell him how much he had helped me with his words of advice. I carried out my remaining assignments feeling relaxed and happy. Everything was now falling into place and I wished that somewhere Aakash would know how thankful I was to him. The happiest of assignments was when I had to visit Colombo. I had notified Aunty Jameela on my impending visit and she had organized a lavish dinner to introduce me to her family and friends. That morning I spent with her, talking about my beloved grandmother, she spoke of their childhood and friendship and filled me with little details of Ummi's life in Mandvi, but even she could not enlighten me on the mysterious young Deepani, Aunty Jameela had never met her. That evening she revelled in her role as hostess, delighted to be introducing me as her niece. I left Colombo feeling that although not by blood, I had family there.

I had been to Africa on a previous assignment but this trip was to be my final obligation before my reign came to a close. I touched down in Nairobi, where I was warmly received and my last assignment was to a nearby village, for the opening of a children's hospital. Little children in their colourful outfits lined the sandy roads to greet me. Their bright beautiful faces beamed, while the sound of cheerful 'Jambo' rang in my ears. I alighted to be greeted by song and dance and was then taken to be introduced to a long line of dignitaries and visitors. On my journey I had hoped, but never really expected, to see him, but suddenly, I spotted him. Although I had only seen his silhouette in the darkness, somehow I knew this was Aakash. He did not recognize me, he looked distracted, I bent to hug a little child who had run up to me, and when I stood up I was being introduced to Aakash Ahamed. I looked him in the eye and remembered my first words to him. Then I asked him if he had given up smoking. When he heard me speak, he looked as if he had been struck by lightning and then he broke into the widest grin I had ever seen.

We met again later that day and we both made sure we could be in touch in the future.

## CHAPTER 22

# SURYA CHANDNI TAARE "WRITTEN IN THE STARS."

I had completed my reign and all that remained was to crown the next title-holder. I bid goodbye to Nisha and happily returned to the loving care of Neelam at my house in Mumbai. My twenty-first birthday had passed, I was alone, independent, and happy. A legal letter awaited me at my house, requesting me to visit their offices at my convenience. A few days later, I complied with the request and was met by an elderly lawyer. He had been entrusted with deeds of the house that had been transferred into my name but, more importantly, a sealed envelope to be handed to me personally once I had reached the age of twenty-one. I returned home with both and opened the envelope.

It was a voice I had yearned to hear, a voice from the past, a long letter written by my loving Ummi.

My beloved child,

"When I was a little child, I hated my name Bhoomi. I remember remonstrating with my mother, as to why I carried this dull name and why she had not named me after "the sun, the moon, or the stars." "Bhoomi," she said, "remember you are a child of the Earth, and never forget that." So when your dear mother placed you in my arms, I named you for everything I yearned for, everything I dreamed of:

Surya, Chandni, Taare, you are "the light of my life."

The letter rambled on, the past came to life, and then finally, it all became clear. I made the connection, the past caught up with the present, the future was yet uncertain.

# CHAPTER 23

# SURYA CHANDNI TAARE
# "OUR PLACE IN THE SUN."

We spoke to each other every day after our second encounter. We spoke about everything, he was so easy to talk to. He confided in me his dreams and ambitions; I, my desire to study. He encouraged me and we made plans. We gradually got to know each other and fell in love. I do not know when or how it transpired but, one day, when we discussed the future, it dawned on us that the future involved us being together.

I had my final night in the limelight and crowned the new 'Miss World.' He completed his internship and was due back in Australia to complete his studies. We arranged to meet, we decided on the place and we set the date.

I checked into the same hotel, this time proudly owning up to my name, and I waited for him. That night, I sat outside at the same terrace beneath a starry sky, the flares burned brightly at a distance, and I did not see him approach. I could smell him before I saw him, that familiar woody fragrance. He wrapped his arms around me as I turned and lifted up my face to meet his lips. There was passion there, as natural as could be. We had both come home.

## CHAPTER 24

# MANDVI

We spent the next few days blissfully happy. There was no doubt in my mind that we were made for each other, and we made each other complete.

We planned our future, he to return to Australia to complete his medical studies, and I to join him there to study as I had wished to do.

We spoke of the past, the unlikely coincidence of us meeting in Mandvi, the likelihood of my beloved Ummi being Bhoomi, the childhood playmate of his grandfather and grand uncle. It was as if we were meant to be together. I told him of my childhood, the mystery of my origin, and the revelation in Ummi's letter.

We planned on what we needed to do in the present.

I called him and he was delighted to hear my voice again. We visited my grand uncle together and gave him Ummi's letter to read. He was overcome with emotion when our relationship was revealed, he embraced me tightly and broke down in tears. I had finally given him the answers and the peace of mind he had sought in his later years.

I called my grandfather at the number I had been given many months before. It was of the young man who handed me the bracelet. He was understandably shocked to hear from me as I requested to speak to his grandfather and mine. The line was clear, the explanations complicated, but eventually he understood. I could hear the sorrow in his voice when he realized the consequences of their tragic love story. He surprised me by announcing he would be flying into Mumbai as soon as he could. He wanted to meet me, he needed to visit his beloved Deepani's grave, he needed to tell her he had returned to take her with him so that he and his precious Deepani could finally rest in peace.

My own father, I had decided, could wait, and sometime after when his children were both adults and when I could lay aside the little resentment I carried, I would contact him and accept him back in my life when I felt ready.

Aakash had informed his parents that he would be staying for a while in India before returning. He had told them he had met a girl in Mandvi. We made arrangements to visit his granduncle in Bhuj, his grandparents were due to be there too. On the morning of our journey, Aakash and I were sitting for an early breakfast when, from across the table, I saw that dumbstruck expression and his now-familiar widest of smiles. He stood up to hug an elegant stately lady accompanied by a tall dignified gentleman. Aakash introduced me, the gentleman did not react with undue surprise but the lady took one look at me and I beheld that same dumbstruck expression and the widest of smiles. I knew immediately that these were his parents.

They had arrived the night before, somewhat anxious about the girl who was keeping their son back in India.

It was a joyous reunion, with me providing the added excitement. I was struck that it was not me being the celebrity that mattered, it was that I was Bhoomi's granddaughter and the strangest of coincidences of Aakash and I meeting up in Mandvi. It was as if the stars had finally aligned to bring us all together. I was fondly embraced and warmly welcomed and, finally, had what I had longed for all my life, a family. I knew Aakash and I would be together, eventually may even be married, and together we could give the happiest of endings to the tragically doomed love stories of my fascinating mother and my beautiful grandmother with the mesmerizing eyes.

# GLOSSARY

**Surya** – Sun

**Chandni** – Moonlight

**Taare** – Star

**Bhoomi** – Earth

**Pani** – Water (Deepani)

**Pavan** – Wind (Pavani)

**Agni** – God of fire (Magni)

**Rowan** – A tree

**Loha** – Iron (Lohan)

**Mehul** – Rain

**Zaaheb** – Gold

**Aakash** – Sky

**Beedi** – A type of cheap cigarette made with unprocessed tobacco wrapped in leaves.

**Dupatta** – A shawl draped over the chest and shoulder

**Veranda** – A roofed platform along the outside of a house, level with the ground floor.

**Sagar** – Sea

**Manzil** – House in Arabic

**Athar** – Perfume

**Gagra** – A type of skirt which is long

**Choli** – A blouse

**Kajal** – A black powder used in South Asia around the eyes

**Sherwani** – Knee-length coat worn by men in South Asia

**Mehendi** – Art of applying temporary henna tattoos especially as a part of a preparation for a wedding

**Nikah** – Marriage contract

**Ghazal** – A lyric poem repeated in rhyme

**Bachcha** – Child

**Kurta** – A loose collarless shirt worn by people in South Asia

**Chappals** – Slippers

**Dabeli** – A popular snack food originating from the Kutch region of Gujrat